THE THICKET

NOELLE W. IHLI

DYNAMITE BOOKS

Published 2021 by Dynamite Books

www.dynamitebookspublishing.com

ISBN: 978-0-5789-4684-9

Any references to historical events, real people, or real places are used fictitiously. Names, characters, and places are products of the author's imagination.

Book design by Dynamite Books.

First printing, 2021.

Dynamite Books, LLC

For Nate, my high-school sweetheart twice removed.

The blond news anchor reveals hardly anything about the two victims except their ages.

But that's all it takes to keep Taylor's phone chirping out text notifications from Maren and Jamie, who are sure that one of the victims went to Minico Middle School. Braden. Or possibly Brandon. Nobody can remember his name.

His sister, Norah, was briefly part of their friend group in middle school. According to Maren, Norah deleted her Facebook profile an hour ago when someone tagged her in the comments section of the breaking story on KQRZ.

Already, 605 people in Rupert, Idaho, have marked themselves "safe" from the incident at the Thicket. The news story has 1,000 shares and nearly as many comments. There are the kids who almost went to the Thicket tonight but had too much homework. There are the frantic parents whose teenager was supposed to be at the Thicket tonight and now isn't responding to texts. There are the wanna-be sleuths posting close-ups of still-frame news footage. There are the creeps who are already insisting that the tragedy is fake news. And there are several people who insist they saw the bodies on the floor of the cabin before anyone realized the blood was real.

Taylor sets her phone to silent and turns on the TV in her room. The news is replaying the same grainy footage of a body bag being loaded into an ambulance. At one point as the camera pans, the flashing lights from the ambulance collide with the strobing light show of the DJ booth at the center of the plaza. For a moment, Taylor's bedroom is bathed in a spray of rainbow beams.

As the blond news anchor—Caroline—repeats the same information about the "horrific tragedy" and "no new information yet," the camera cuts to the facade of a dark cabin. The open door yawns like a mouth. First responders duck beneath the crime scene tape then disappear inside.

Caroline reassures viewers that the glinting blood on the exterior walls of the cabin isn't real, but rather part of the decor at the Thicket.

Taylor wonders how Caroline can tell the difference.

Her stomach clenches a little tighter as she pulls her bedspread closer around her shoulders and imagines what the real blood—on the inside of the cabin—must look like. She glances at the lock screen of her phone and reads the latest text from Jamie. *Does this mean they're gonna close the whole thing down?* It's followed by a frowny emoji.

Taylor frowns too and reaches for the remote to turn off the TV. She'll text Maren and Jamie back in the morning. But before she climbs into bed, she logs into Facebook and marks herself safe — then double-checks the lock on her bedroom window. She's being silly, she chides herself. The person who brought a knife into the Thicket is almost certainly not outside her bedroom window right now. She's just feeling anxious after watching the news.

But then again, he's somewhere.

CHAPTER 1

5 hours earlier

"Whatcha been sneaking down to the boiler room, Freddy?" Norah's brother Brandon points a finger in the direction of the short and slightly overweight Freddy Krueger who is standing directly in his path with an unreadable expression.

Brandon puffs out his stomach and pats it. "Love those Twinkies, huh?"

Norah puts her head down in embarrassment and keeps walking, hoping Brandon will follow. "He's not really Freddy Krueger," she hisses in Brandon's ear as she passes. "Stop being a jerk."

A group of kids just ahead of them have stopped to watch the standoff. One boy snickers as Norah trips over a crack in the floor, and one of the girls sends a withering glance at Norah, then shifts her glare to Brandon. "Asshole," she mutters to the two girls beside her, zipping her pink bomber jacket tighter and smacking her thickly glossed lips. "Come on, let's walk faster."

A blast of steam shoots out of the wall beside Norah with a high-pitched whistle, and she screams, feeling her face burn red. She hears another ripple of laughter from the group ahead.

For the hundredth time, Norah regrets agreeing to take her brother to the Thicket tonight. Not that she'd had much of a choice. Brandon somehow knew that Norah had not only skipped last period on Friday but that she'd also spent the stolen hour smoking weed with a couple of juniors from Raft River.

So basically he's blackmailing her.

"Bitch," Brandon calls after the group ahead of them as he finally gives up on getting a reaction out of Freddy. He says it quietly enough that the girl and her friends probably won't hear the insult above the other screams and a new blast of steam from the wall.

Norah turns around and tries to set a faster pace, leading the way through the big, red-lit cabin that has been modeled after a boiler room.

More rapid-fire blasts of warm steam shoot through the cool air that smells like pavement after a storm. More bogeymen from *Freddy's Nightmare*—these ones robotic— pop out from dark corners. Norah bites back a scream each time, and she finally looks behind her to see what's taking Brandon so long.

He's meandering slower than ever.

"Can you please hurry up?" she shouts back to him, exasperated and on edge. Haunted houses have never been her cup of tea, but Brandon is obsessed. She stands where she is in the dark room, gritting her teeth at the chaos, waiting until Brandon is finally within earshot.

"Wasn't Jace's mom supposed to drive you here tonight? What happened to your actual friends?" she explodes when he is a few steps away.

She feels the sting of the words before they are even out of her mouth. She knows they will dig at her obnoxious but sensitive little brother. Part of her wants to apologize. To ruffle his hair like she used to and try to enjoy their time together. And the other part—the bigger part—just feels mean and annoyed.

Brandon's jaw tightens, but he doesn't look at her. Instead, he studies the metal pipes that snake up the concrete walls, dripping tiny rivulets of water onto the floor below. Just ahead, there is a glowing furnace. It belches out what looks like hot coals—and bone fragments.

Norah clenches her jaw. "Can we at least move faster? It's gross in here."

If anything, Brandon just walks slower. "How long do you think Mom and Dad would ground you for if I told them about *your* friends?" he says.

Someone wearing a black coat and mask brushes past Norah in the dark, and she involuntarily yelps yet again. She's had enough. "I said I would *bring* you here. I didn't say I'd walk through this freak show all night."

She points to a dimly glowing exit sign a few yards to their right. "I'm waiting in the plaza."

Norah stomps toward the exit sign without looking back at him, so she won't see whether he has a sneer or a wounded look on his baby face.

She can already feel the anger evaporating as she pushes her way through a wooden exit door and proceeds along the wooded trail that promises to lead her back to the plaza.

Ten minutes later, the volume of the thumping music from the DJ booth tells her she's almost there. It's still mostly light out. The monsters roaming through the plaza aren't nearly as scary as they are in the wooded trails and cabins. The smell of mini donuts makes her mouth water.

Norah decides she will get the largest pack of donuts they have. The kind with cinnamon and sugar. She'll save some for Brandon.

CHAPTER 2

Brandon pretends to study the pipes, the furnace, anything until he's sure Norah is gone. For the hundredth time, he wishes he hadn't come here at all.

Andrew had sent out a group text fifteen minutes before Brandon was supposed to leave for the Thicket.

Sorry, bros. 2 much homework.

Five minutes later, Brandon's phone had pinged again. Cole. Then Jace, whose mom was supposed to chauffeur.

So he'd blackmailed Norah into taking him. If his mom knew that Jace and the others had ditched him, she'd make him go to that stupid "Buddies" workshop during lunch again. The one he'd been forced to attend last year when he cried like a dumb baby after some kids wrote "skid mark" in permanent marker on his locker two days into the school year.

Screw Andrew and Jace and Cole. Tomorrow at school he'd tell everyone in first period how he'd walked through the Thicket alone and wasn't even scared. He'd leave out the fact that it was still mostly light out and that he'd conned his sister into taking him. The Thicket made the list of "10 Scariest Haunted Houses in the United States" on SocialBuzz every year. People would be impressed.

As Brandon reaches the exit to Cabin Nine, the boiler room, he hears a piercing chorus of screams coming from somewhere down the trail. The sun has dipped down a little more, and the shadows from the thick trees are getting longer. He hadn't anticipated how massive the Thicket would be, despite his classmates' assertions. The marked trail connecting the network of haunted cabins cuts a path through thick underbrush, pine trees, and dense stands of aspens. In the summer, when the elaborate props are dismantled and the generators are gone, the Thicket is a popular hiking spot.

A few feet off the trail, a branch snaps with a quiet pop.

Brandon stops walking but keeps his face neutral in case it's Norah returning with a change of heart.

When he doesn't hear anything else—except a cacophony of screams coming from somewhere in the distance—he feels his stomach clench. Why couldn't Andrew have texted earlier? Why was everyone else suddenly busy at the last minute too?

The knot in his stomach clenches harder. Did any of them actually like him? Was this year different? He had homeroom with all three boys. They'd laughed last week when Brandon stuck the peanut-butter-and-jam side of his sandwich to the whiteboard while Ms. Leavitt had her back turned. And the day after that, Cole had dared him to take down a few of the magnetic letters on the classroom door to turn "Welcome to Our Class" to "Welcome to ur ass." He'd done it.

"They like me," he mutters quietly under his breath and forces himself to keep walking along the trail littered with fallen leaves. But he can't help but wonder if Jace, Andrew, and Cole are together right now. Playing video games at Andrew's house while they eat pizza. Laughing at the fact that Brandon is at the Thicket alone.

Brandon pushes the thoughts away and peers through the thick trees lining the trail to his right. He decides he'll be nicer to Norah when he finally reaches the exit to the plaza. Do the corn maze with her like she wanted. Stop being a jerk. He suddenly remembers the $20 his mom gave him—to buy treats for himself and the other boys. He feels around in his pocket for the wrinkled bill and decides he will buy one of everything in the plaza. *Then* find Norah.

As Brandon comes around the next bend in the trail, he finally sees the next looming structure—a decrepit barn with one side nearly caved in. The planks of wood holding the structure together are bowing and splintering under the strain.

When Brandon pushes aside the rickety door, the acrid smell makes his nostrils flare. He covers his nose with his jacket. Does fake blood smell that way?

The room is suspiciously quiet. And dark.

As he takes another step forward, the lights suddenly flash on, and the room erupts into motion.

 Half of a cow carcass, spotted skin still attached to its body, is jerking violently against the side of the inner wall, making a wet thumping sound. Hanging from the ceiling from enormous meat hooks are more carcasses, glistening red, swinging as they're pulled back and forth by a series of metal wires.

Brandon jumps and swears under his breath, then he quickly looks behind him.

When nothing else leaps out at him, he walks past the swinging carcasses and leans forward to study the half-butchered cow hanging against the wall. The detail is pretty awesome. Gnarled, black-and-white whorls of hair are streaked with smears of manure. And there are actual flies swarming across the jagged, bloody slashes near the head. He can hear them buzzing.

He squints closer, wondering how they get the flies to stay. He's maybe a foot away when he realizes that the "flies" are coming from a tiny projector in the corner of the room, its beam of light masked by the strobing of the spotlights on the carcasses.

In the distance, Brandon hears a long, rattling scream, followed by a loud thumping noise.

He looks behind him, then ahead. Still nobody.

Pulling his phone out of his pocket, he snaps a photo of the cow's half-closed, swollen eye covered in flies. Then he sends it to Jace without a caption. *There.*

Pocketing the phone, Brandon moves toward a swath of dirty sheets hanging from the ceiling of the barn, midway through the slaughterhouse. When he pushes the sheets aside, he sees that the strobing lights are gone, replaced by a dim, flickering bulb in the center of the dark room. Lining the walls and the cement pathway are cages full of twitching chickens. Some are missing beaks. Some legs. Some, their entire heads. The floor is covered in a thick layer of white feathers and stained red with blood.

A big guy wearing overalls and a burlap sack covering his face is standing in the corner of the room. He's positioned just behind the furthest row of cages, and he is holding a glinting ax.

The guy takes a step toward Brandon. The front of his overalls is covered with more of the white feathers—and dark splotches of blood. Two eyeholes and a ragged mouth have been cut into the burlap sack.

He smiles, revealing jagged, haphazard teeth. Then he bellows like an ox and rushes toward Brandon, holding the ax over his head.

Brandon exhales hard and forces himself to stay where he is. "You can't touch me," he scoffs loudly, relieved when his voice doesn't crack.

The guy stops just short of where Brandon is standing, the bellowing scream tapering into a wheedling moan. With one gloved hand, soaked through with red liquid, he points to the twitching chickens on the floor then back at Brandon. He waves the ax back and forth with his free hand.

Brandon lifts both middle fingers and stares back at the actor, adrenaline prickling its way down his back. *It's all fake.* All he has to do is remember that. A smile tugs at the corner of his mouth as the guy slowly lowers the ax then turns and walks back to the corner of the room, pointing to the exit.

"That's right," Brandon calls behind him and walks through another swath of sheets into the next room.

This room is smaller and more brightly lit. In front of him is a sawhorse dining table set with tin cups and plates as well as a red-checked tablecloth. Facing away from him, a woman sits slumped in her chair, face down. There is an ax handle buried between the loose apron strings on her back.

Brandon takes a wary step forward.

When the woman doesn't jump up, he takes a quick photo of the ax head wedged into her spine. He sends this photo to Cole. Then, pocketing the phone again, he walks through the exit door and back into the gathering twilight.

This night hasn't been so bad after all.

CHAPTER 3

The body in the grimy bathtub lurches, sending a ripple through the brackish water. The man's protruding intestines slap lazily against the filthy porcelain.

Plap, plap, plap.

Spencer sighs and resists the urge to pick at a new rash of acne on his chin.

The mechanics at the Thicket are good this year. When the guy in the bathtub—Spencer calls him "Norman"—writhes around every thirty seconds, the motion is just the right mix of jerky and smooth.

On opening day, he'd heard more than one kid shriek that the effects were "freaking amazing."

Spencer shifts on his heels to crouch a little lower, trying to ease the strain on his stinging calves. At 6'4', his frame barely fits inside the broken cabinet where he is now stooped, waiting to leap out at the kids as they shuffle through the cabin in sparse, tight clusters.

It's coming up on 7:30 pm. Still mostly light out. This means he's only seen a couple dozen kids on the trails. Like last year, the surge on opening day has dwindled to a trickle after only a week or so. The lull will last until the beginning of October, especially during the slow hours between opening and sunset.

Spencer understands. While the temperature is still hovering near seventy and dim light is still filtering through the chinks in the rough log walls, he's just a too-tall kid in a costume. And Norman is just a machine, rolling around in fake blood.

When the sun goes down, it's different.

The robot lurches again on cue, its pulpy face pitching to the right, mouth open wide, back arching out of the pool of blood and guts. Norman has gone off at least a hundred times now, for an audience of one.

Spencer tries shifting his weight to one leg, letting the other leg slide over the splintering edge of the cupboard so it's at least partially extended.

As the sound of high-pitched laughter and muffled, thudding footsteps drift into earshot, Spencer quickly draws his left foot back into the cupboard. He rocks forward onto the balls of his feet, careful not to jostle the cabinet door.

It sounds like a bigger group. Maybe tonight will pick up after all.

As the swinging door creaks open, the laughter goes quiet. By design, the kids' eyes are drawn first to the bathtub. Even in the partial light filtering through the doorway of the cabin, Spencer knows he is nearly invisible crouched inside the frame of the decrepit cabinet.

"Oh my god," the first kid shrieks as Norman abruptly thrashes to life in the bloody bathtub water, right on cue. "Whoa." The last part tumbles out with a delighted laugh. It's just a prop.

Even though Spencer has witnessed this reaction dozens of times over the past week, he smiles. Norman is pretty cool. And pretty realistic. And unlike most of the kids who walk through the swinging door to the ramshackle cabin, Spencer has seen Norman up close. Even his eyes—down to the bloodshot whites and the glassy red corneas—look real.

Three girls, cell phones held in front of them like shields, follow the boy into the room. Unsurprisingly, they're a few years younger than the usual crowd. Spencer has even seen a few elementary-age kids this year—while it's light out, anyway. He made the mistake of jumping out at one the week before, which got him a lecture from management.

In tandem, the kids scan the room for more surprises. Then, thinking they are alone with the gruesome robot, they huddle together in front of the bathtub for a selfie as the phone camera flashes go off, one by one.

The nearest girl's ankle is just a few inches from Spencer's right hand. Stylishly threadbare jeans and twee plaid flats with the soles half-covered in mud.

Spencer keeps his hand tucked against his chest, thinking of his supervisor, a loud, short woman with wide-set eyes and an androgynous haircut. *You can't touch the guests, and they can't touch you,* she'd repeated, wagging her finger back and forth between herself and the staffers at least twenty times during orientation.

Shifting back onto his heels, Spencer drums up a rattling moan in the back of his throat. Quiet at first. Then louder, harsher. The girls stop taking selfies and call out to the boy, who is almost out the back of the cabin. "Do you hear—"

Just as Norman springs back to life again in the bathtub, Spencer bangs one hand hard against the plywood cabinet, sending the crooked door flying against the wall behind him with a hollow smack. Then, careful not to bang his head on the top of the cupboard—it happened once last week—he leaps upright.

The girl in the plaid flats jumps as if she has just been electrocuted, scrambling backward against her friends. All four kids scream at exactly the same pitch. The boy, who has doubled back through the open exit door, trips over the taped-down wiring that leads from the cabin to a generator tucked behind it. He gasps loudly as he scrambles to his feet again, eyes wide.

"Holy crap, that mask is creepy," the kid exclaims, unhurt and clearly impressed. He takes a step closer, trying to get a glimpse of Spencer's eyes inside the dark sockets. They all do this.

Spencer takes another slow, sinister step forward. He reminds himself to check the generator connection on Norman once the kids crash out of the shed and disappear down the trail.

When he's about a foot away, he stomps his foot and lurches forward. The girls scatter past him, squealing in delight this time.

Spencer counts the seconds as he folds himself back into the cupboard. Norman goes off once, twice, three times. The connection is fine.

Exhaling, Spencer repositions himself against the scratchy plywood, checking the time on his cell phone before crouching down on his heels. It's 7:34. Still half an hour until sunset.

He lifts up the edge of his mask to prod at the tiny red bumps on his chin again. He wonders absently if he might be allergic to latex.

Thinking better of touching the inflamed skin, he curls his fingers back into a fist, running a hand lightly over the contours of the mask he's wearing instead. A sleek, sharp beak juts out in the front. The beak curves downward over his nose and mouth, nearly reaching his chin. The only other embellishment on the mask is a thick line of metal rivets surrounding the gaping black eye sockets.

Originally, he thought the stark black mask was supposed to be some kind of bird. A crow, maybe. But when his girlfriend Dana saw it, she told him it was an old-fashioned medical mask, meant to hold flowers and other good-smelling stuff for medieval doctors who traveled from town to town, treating victims of the plague. To hide the smell of death.

When several minutes pass without any sign of another group of kids approaching, Spencer gives up crouching and sits down, letting both feet hang outside the cabinet door. He's going to get a Charley horse if he sits like this much longer.

Most of the time he can hear the kids coming a mile away, exclaiming about how they're going to pull the next guy's mask off, or how many bags of cotton candy they can eat by the time they have to leave, or who just made out with who in the corn maze.

He'll have plenty of time to get back into position.

Except he doesn't.

Spencer doesn't realize he's closed his eyes until he feels, rather than sees, that someone has not only entered the room but is standing in front of the cabinet.

It takes a few seconds for his eyes to focus on the shape in front of him through the cabinet's partially open crooked door.

It's a man. He's wearing a mask too, one of the generic blood-and-guts latex faces. Bloody lips peel back over bloody teeth. The mask has bulging yellow eyes and a thick, bulbous nose.

The man is tall. Almost as tall as Spencer. He's dressed in loose-fitting army fatigues and a heavy black coat that seems out of place with the faint sunlight still streaming through the door at the other end of the cabin.

He's standing close enough that Spencer isn't sure how to gracefully get to his feet in the cabinet again, let alone jump out.

The man has seen him, anyway.

Pushing the cabinet door open until it just grazes the man's pant leg, Spencer shifts one foot beneath him.

The guy doesn't move.

"I like your mask." The man's voice is soft, almost feminine. It's disconcertingly at odds with his hulking frame and the mask's grinning, bloodstained lips.

Spencer glances toward the entrance of the cabin as he shifts his other foot beneath him, hoping nobody else is watching this strange exchange.

Nobody is.

The man shuffles back just slightly as Spencer moves to stand. And when he speaks again, Spencer can see his real lips moving inside the puckered, stitched mouth hole of the mask. "I said, I like your mask."

And yours is boring, Spencer thinks, annoyed now. Drawing himself upright and trying to muster some kind of authority, he points toward the exit. The opportunity for a scare has passed. He'll punt on this one.

The kids that tramp through the woods and the cabins are, without fail, annoying. But the adults are usually worse.

The man doesn't budge. If anything, he's leaning forward, closer to Spencer. "Will you let me try your mask on?"

Spencer opens his mouth, ready to break character. He didn't sign up for this. And another group of kids will walk through the door any second now.

In the bathtub, Norman bolts upright as the dark water laps back and forth against his grimy toes.

"Hey, man, if you'll just exit that—"

Spencer closes his mouth as the guy pulls something out of the inner pocket of his thick black jacket.

It's a long knife.

Spencer looks for the telltale glint of plastic. *They can't touch you.* Then he takes a step sideways, still unwilling to give ground. "I'm sorry, I'm going to have to ask you to—"

Behind the latex mouth, the man's real lips stretch into a smile. "I'm going to try it on now."

CHAPTER 4

Norah pops a cinnamon-sugar donut into her mouth whole, deciding she will eat two more and save the rest for Brandon. Her phone pings, and she feels a little spark of excitement when she sees the reply from Aaron—the junior from Raft River who knew where to find pot. The excitement is followed by a pang of guilt.

Sry. Ur brother sounds like a D.

Bored and still annoyed, Norah had sent Aaron a text complaining about Brandon and his lack of social skills. It's not like her. She's always been the first to defend her brother, despite how obnoxious he can be. Brandon doesn't have an official diagnosis, but she's quietly convinced he might be on the spectrum.

Norah wipes her hands on her jeans, tucks her phone back into her sweatshirt, and scans the dusky plaza. A symphony of screams that rise and fall across the plaza and from inside the trail maze has become part of the background noise. The screams rise and fall, becoming the undercurrent for the chaotic music the DJ is playing on a loop from the center of the plaza. Every few minutes, a chainsaw starts to buzz, eliciting more screams, then laughter.

Norah wonders idly if the security guard in the tan uniform and hat she saw earlier has been trained to tell whether someone actually needs help or not. From where Norah sits, all the screaming sounds the same.

Shaking the thought aside, she texts Aaron back and eats another donut. There's plenty left. And as soon as Brandon appears from the exit, he'll eat the rest without so much as a thank-you.

CHAPTER 5

While Brandon walks, he pulls his phone out of his pocket to see if Jace or Cole has replied. There's nothing. Somewhere behind him, he hears a distant series of rapid-fire screams, followed by the blare of a car horn.

The trail has turned narrow, winding through a thick grove of elms then across an empty creek bed. The remains of an old stone fence run parallel to the rocky ground, blocking the rest of the trails from view. Finally, the path opens up to yet another small structure, this one a smaller cabin with a basic log facade.

As Brandon approaches the entrance, he can see dark liquid seeping from beneath the half-open doorway, dripping onto the dirt trail and staining it a sickly black. From just inside he hears muffled, frantic splashing and loud gurgling noises.

It's not real, he reminds himself, feeling the knot in his stomach yield just a little. He decides that whatever is inside, he'll take one last photo to send to Andrew. Screw those guys anyway.

He's glad he stayed tonight after all. SocialBuzz was right. Aside from that porky Freddy Krueger, the Thicket is legit this year.

From fifty yards behind him, in the farmhouse, Brandon hears more squeals of terror. "Speaking of oinkers," he murmurs, liking the sound of it. "Bunch of oinkers," he whispers again, making a mental note to use the phrase at school. Maybe about Mrs. Leavitt.

As Brandon walks through the threshold of the doorway, stepping over the dark swaths of liquid in the dirt, a sudden movement draws his eye to the left.

There's a large, dingy clawfoot tub in the corner.

A man, whose face has been almost completely hacked away, is writhing on the floor of the tub, sloshing the water back and forth. Each movement sends tiny brown waves back and forth over his feet. His intestines, limp gray curls, are floating just above his stomach in the brackish water.

Blood gurgles from his nose and mouth.

"Ungh," the bloody figure gurgles, flopping against the edge of the tub toward Brandon, making some of the water splash out of the tub.

A few drops of liquid land on the sleeve of Brandon's sweatshirt.

Despite himself, he takes one step backward at the sound the man is making. The air has a foul, metallic tang to it, and he wonders if it's coming from the liquid that's pooling at the bottom of the tub.

The rest of the room is quiet and nondescript. The only sound is the bubbling liquid on the man's lips and the wet flopping noises.

Brandon stares at the man in the bathtub for a few seconds, wondering whether there will be more to the performance. But after a few seconds, the feeble thrashing stops and his head lolls to the side.

Brandon pulls his phone out of his pocket and snaps a photo of the man's face, this one for Andrew. Then he takes another step into the cabin. On the floor a few feet away from the tub is a dusty, broken-looking cabinet with its door hanging by one hinge.

In the dim light, Brandon can see that another figure, a second man, is concealed partway inside the cabinet.

Brandon waits for the man to jump out. When nothing happens, he steps a little closer.

Something about the position of the man's legs is wrong.

Brandon steps even closer and tentatively tugs at the cabinet door to open it all the way.

The slumped figure is covered in blood, his head tilted back and to the side so that his chin juts out in front of him, defiant and a little cocky. What's visible of his blood-spattered, grimacing face is obscured by tufts of long brown hair, blocking his eyes.

Brandon's gaze follows the bloody form down to its feet, where a long, copper wire peeks out of one shoe. He cautiously reaches out to touch the man's visible chin.

Plastic.

It's a robot. And it appears to be broken.

Brandon shakes his head as the guy in the bathtub thrashes around a little more.

A quiet scuffling noise suddenly draws Brandon's attention to the furthest corner of the shack. Caught off guard, he braces and peers forward. Most of the cabins along the trail have had just one real scarer and one or more robots. This tiny cabin has two.

The second scarer dressed in black takes a step toward him. He's wearing a simple mask with deep-set eyeholes and a sharp, bulging beak. A creepy bird, maybe. Metal rivets flash in the dim light as the figure takes a step forward.

Of everything Brandon has seen tonight, this room shouldn't be that scary. But he feels his stomach coil tight.

"Do you like my mask?"

Brandon furrows his brows. This is the first time one of the staff members has spoken to him. And he is suddenly annoyed. It ruins the effect a little.

"That guy's mask is better," Brandon retorts, pointing to the man in the bathtub, whose thrashing has become more erratic.

Brandon turns to look at the bathtub behind him. He suddenly notices that there are thin copper wires sticking out of the pool of dark blood in the bathtub, too. However, the wires don't seem to be connected to anything.

Puzzled, he turns to look back at the robot in the cabinet. When he glances up, he sees that the scarer in the beaked mask has crossed half the distance between them.

As Brandon watches, the scarer uses one gloved hand to pull a long knife from within his coat.

The weapon isn't that impressive compared to the ax in the slaughterhouse, but there is something different about the way the figure in the beaked mask holds it.

"Do you wish you had a mask like his?" The masked scarer points at the scarer thrashing in the bathtub.

His voice is quiet, gentle even.

Run, insists a voice in the back of Brandon's head. But he tells the voice to shut up and takes a step forward toward the man holding the knife.

"It's not that great," Brandon says, walking toward the exit a few feet away.

That's when he feels the tip of the knife run lightly over the back of his jacket. Just a gentle, dragging pressure over the denim.

They can't touch you.

Anger flares through him along with a new kind of fear that doesn't ask but rather tells this time.

Run.

So he does.

But not quickly enough to avoid the knife as it cuts through the back of his hoodie with a slick ripping sound and searing, white-hot pain.

At first, he can't scream.

Can't move.

And when the first scream does tear through his throat, he knows it's loud enough that everyone will hear it.

But no one will come.

CHAPTER 6

Norah reaches for the cardboard tray to pick up one of the last remaining mini donuts, then puts her hand back in her lap. She can already feel her stomach starting to complain at what she's eaten in the past forty minutes while waiting for Brandon to emerge from the trails.

She pulls out her phone and stares hard at the text she sent him twenty minutes ago, hoping to see the three little dots appear at the bottom. But there is nothing.

Norah squints through the smoky darkness at the group of kids walking toward her. She's pretty sure she recognizes the girl with the bomber jacket and lip gloss. Everyone in the group is holding funnel cakes and caramel apples. That means they've been out of the trail maze long enough to wait in line at the Snak Shak across the plaza by the corn maze where Norah bought the donuts earlier.

Norah watches the group of kids until they disappear into the darkness of the dusky plaza. The aroma of sizzling dough and sugar manages to mostly mask the ever-present smell coming from the corn syrup factory just a few miles away. But above the tree line, she can still make out the distant outline of the factory, where steady puffs of white smoke are drifting skyward.

It's the smell that dooms Declo to a population of about 500 most of the year. The Wind River Sugar factory acts as a magnet of sorts for the locals willing to overlook the cloying stench—employing nearly 70 percent of the rural Idaho town, including Norah's dad. It repels pretty much everybody else.

Halloween is the notable exception to the rule. Every year, Declo's infamous Thicket with its wooded trails and bordering cornfields draws kids from all over Idaho, Utah, and even Colorado and Washington.

Norah's attention shifts to a stout security guard wearing a tan uniform. The light-colored fabric highlights the dark circles under his arms as he passes beneath a strobing light. He looks young. Norah's gaze automatically shifts to his hip. He doesn't have a gun, which confirms what Kenny—Aaron's friend who sometimes joined them to smoke—told her. Kenny had worked as a scarer at the Thicket last fall after school and claimed that there was no actual security experience required. Just a tan hat, tan shirt, and an official-looking pin-on badge.

Norah watches as the wannabe guard smiles at two girls who are trying to snap a selfie with a hooded grim reaper standing at the entrance to the trails. The reaper is blocking the gap between the hay bale walls with a scythe to prevent anyone from skipping the line.

While the girls are focused on perfecting the photo angle, the guard motions to one of the other scarers—who is dressed as a toothy werewolf. The werewolf weaves through the sparse line until he's right behind the girls. When the wolf pounces into the girls' photo, they drop the phone with an ear-splitting scream, nearly colliding with the hooded grim reaper.

Norah smiles slightly and turns her gaze back to the exit of the trails, where another huddle of kids is emerging. She can't hear what they're saying over the thumping music and the rise and fall of screaming kids running through the plaza.

She almost follows the guard in the tan outfit as he turns to walk the perimeter of the plaza but decides she'll wait ten more minutes. She's being silly. Brandon is being Brandon, and it's his own fault the few donuts that remain will be cold.

* * *

Norah waits twenty more minutes before tossing out the last of the cold, waxy donuts. The temperature has dropped with the sun, and she knows that Brandon is wearing only his ratty, thin Aquaman hoodie.

Norah makes her way across the park to an Airstream trailer where a woman with a pink mohawk and red eyeshadow is taking tickets.

The line is a bit longer now, and Norah hovers in the yellow glow of the trailer's light until the woman with the pink hair finishes her transaction. There's a large map of the Thicket plastered across the side of the trailer, boasting "Biggest Haunted Attraction in the USA." Norah counts twenty log cabins marked on the trail map, each with its own creepy name. "The Slaughterhouse." "The Kill Floor." A callout that reads "310 full acres!" is overlaid across the map of the corn maze. She tries to imagine how big 310 acres is but can't. She feels the first tendrils of guilt for leaving Brandon on the trail.

The woman with the pink mohawk directs Norah to wait on a bench outside the trailer, and a few minutes later a guy who introduces himself as the head security guard—Dave— appears. Dave is wearing what appears to be an actual police uniform and a badge but no gun. He listens patiently while Norah tells him about Brandon.

Norah is interrupted twice by the radio clipped to Dave's jacket blinking green, spitting static. *Kid crying . . . ticket booth . . . too scary . . . Trying to get a hold of the parents . . . couple teens peeing on the props . . . bringing them up front.*

Dave is not unkind when he points to the map that Norah has already seen and tells her that the Thicket is a big place. This week he's tracked down more than half a dozen middle schoolers who hadn't quite found their way out of the maze by the time their parents arrived. Still, he tells her he will have one of his security guards do a walkthrough with Brandon's description.

Ten minutes later, the portly guard Norah saw earlier—the one with the pit stains and tan uniform—trudges toward the Airstream from the plaza. He takes a sip of water from the water pouch tucked beneath his thick polyester shirt. Dave explains Norah's concerns then heads back inside the trailer. Norah realizes she's been handed off.

The big guard with the armpit stains, who introduces himself as Bill, talks a mile a minute as he leads the way through the thumping plaza. Norah follows on his heels, still clutching the cold donuts, struggling to hear what he's saying over the chaos.

"I'm supposed to keep security pretty low-key outside the plaza. That's why we have the staff trails," he explains. "People come here to be freaked out, you know? When they see too many clowns in uniform," he grins and points to his own chest, "the killer clowns don't seem as scary, you know?"

Norah doesn't respond, but Bill keeps going. "Not that I'm dying to get out on the trails. One of the guys out there got punched *twice* last year. Kids get strung out on cotton candy and adrenaline and things get wild sometimes."

Norah laughs awkwardly, only half hearing what the guard is saying while she scans the plaza for Brandon. For a second she thinks she sees the back of his blue and teal hoodie at a cotton candy stand. Her heart leaps even as she prepares to tell him how selfish he's been. It's been an hour now.

The kid in the hoodie turns to laugh at someone behind him. It's not Brandon. Norah checks her phone again. Nothing.

Bill is still talking. "I mean, that's the official line from management. Personally, I think we could use a few more guards. This early in the season, it's really just me and an old fart who gets to sit on a bench outside the corn maze. *I* do all the walking."

That explains the pit stains, Norah thinks.

She follows Bill to the same bench she was sitting at earlier. He'll "take a peek" along a few of the staff trails, he assures her. *Hang tight. Stay right here. It'll take some time. Call the number on this card if your brother shows up. It'll route you to the ticket booth. Service is spotty on the trails, but the boss has a radio.*

As Bill walks away, Norah pulls out her phone one more time, hoping that she will see a text. That she can report it's all been a misunderstanding. That Brandon is on the other side of the plaza waiting in line for a corn dog. But there is nothing.

Now that it's finally dark, the plaza has come to life. Everywhere Norah looks there are small groups of kids gleefully squealing, taking selfies, or hurrying toward the next attraction. Just before Bill slips through a nearly invisible blind in the hay bales, an ear-splitting chorus of staccato screams pierce the air to his right.

Norah watches him pause to glance in the direction of the screams while he takes a sip from his CamelBak. Then he turns left and disappears from view.

CHAPTER 7

The man in the beaked mask looks at the body on the floor. Shaggy, dirty-blond hair curls over the boy's ears. Too-short jeans reveal skinny white ankles. And a deep red puddle at the nape of his neck is slowly seeping down the back of his thin blue hoodie.

He can hear the next group of kids coming down the path. They're nearly at the cabin now.

But it doesn't matter. He has time.

The boy will be easier to lift than the staff member. He can't weigh more than a hundred pounds. But the man in the beaked mask decides to leave him where he is lying, face down on the cement floor, adjacent to the cabin's exit.

The babbling voices are nearly at the doorway now.

He wipes a bloody hand on his pants leg and leans against the far wall, turning away from the boy and toward the newcomers.

Darkness is falling quickly now. The kids cast long shadows in the gray light as they step inside the cabin. They move tentatively at first, then crane their necks as they bunch in front of the bathtub.

They ignore the body just a few yards in front of them on the floor. "Oh my god, this one looks real," the first girl exclaims, burying her nose in the collar of a puffy white coat. "It even smells real. What is that?"

He glances at the brackish, bloody water in the bathtub. The body is still now, its head lolling down against its chest.

Drying blood cakes the face, hair, and ears. The portion of his shirt above the water line is already beginning to dry and darken.

There are more voices from the trail, another group. Traffic is picking up.

Taking a step toward the bathtub, the man in the mask lifts the bloody knife in front of him, letting one shoe drag along the concrete with a quiet scraping sound.

The boy at the front of the group of four chokes out a yelp and takes a step back. When he recovers, he laughs. "Damn, I didn't even see that guy."

The girl in the white coat, who is still holding her nose in front of the bathtub, grabs his arm with her free hand and hurries him past the body on the floor, toward the cabin's exit. "Come on you guys!" she calls to the couple behind her who laugh and rush past him. They brush close enough that her white coat flaps against the wet knife, leaving a smear of dark red.

He follows them out of the shack, and they shriek with delight, walking backward to watch him as he raises the knife above his head. He stomps toward them erratically, miming stabbing motions as they scatter in front of him.

The group disappears down the trail, toward the next attraction. He lets his arm fall to his side, watching them until he can just make out their silhouettes.

Behind him, he can hear the rise and fall of new shrieks inside the cabin. New exclamations of terror and glee as they see the bathtub, the body lying on the ground, and the blood that covers nearly every part of the dirt floor.

Keeping his mask on, he follows the trail away from the cabin. Just past the aspens, a stone's throw from the worn dirt footpath, he sees what he is looking for. The dim outline of a tiny white "Staff Only" sign. It's almost invisible, unless you know what you're looking for.

Wiping his hands on his pants again, he tucks the knife into the inner pocket of his coat and ducks through the brush next to the sign, revealing a narrow side trail.

In the distance, he can see dim flashes of light coming from the main plaza. Soft, smoky yellow beams from the headlights of the food trucks. And strobing, fluorescent bursts of light from the DJ booth that pulse in time like the faint bass rhythm of a heartbeat. As he gets closer, he can smell caramel corn beneath the ever-present stink of the corn syrup factory.

He's almost there when he hears the crunch of footsteps approaching along the narrow exit trail, coming from the direction of the plaza.

He considers turning around, taking a different staff exit. If he doubles back, he'll find another one further along the trail. But why? Instead, he stuffs his bloody gloves into his coat pockets and walks faster.

A few seconds later, a stout twenty-something wearing a collared tan shirt and a wide-brimmed tan security hat appears around the bend in front of him. The guard has his head down while he studies the radio in his hand.

For a moment, he thinks the guard will walk right past. But as he approaches, the guard looks up and sees him, inhaling sharply. Then he lets out the breath in a loud whoosh that separates his ample lips. "Jesus, Spencer. You nearly gave me a heart attack." He laughs, adjusting the tan hat that has fallen slightly to the side of his head as he looks back down at the radio and continues walking.

The man in the beaked mask turns and watches through the deep-set eyeholes as the guard's crunching footsteps fade into the darkness of the Thicket.

He considers that maybe he should have stayed a little longer after all, even with the growing crowds. It could be all night before anyone notices that something is amiss in Cabin Twelve.

He gently brushes the idea aside and continues walking.

Caution is the better part of any undertaking. Including murder.

The plaza is filling up with dark silhouettes. The ticket line already stretches beyond his view, into the parking lot. The screams come from every direction now. Short, long. Delighted, pained. High-pitched and trilling, deep and barking.

As he steps through a blind in the hay, a girl wearing a unicorn mask stops to watch. She peers at him expectantly in the smoky darkness.

He growls and lunges toward her, just close enough to brush the tip of her swinging ponytail with his gloved hand. She turns on her heel and squeals, bolting away from him to catch up with her friends.

He watches her go. Then walks toward the ticket trailer at the entrance, through the middle of the plaza.

As he passes near a crackling orange fire barrel sending popping sparks onto the jackets of the kids huddled around it, two teenage boys wolf-whistle at him. When he ignores them, they turn back to the fire. They are laughing, miming as if they will push one another into the barrel.

He continues toward the cluster of food trucks. When he passes through the headlights, a few of the kids standing in line crane their necks to get a better look at his mask. One girl jumps out of his path with a yelp, grinning sheepishly when he doesn't react. Most of the kids, however, ignore him.

He's not the only monster here, after all.

Fifty yards to his right, in the pulsing lights of the DJ booth, a clown with long, yellow teeth and a thick ax through the middle of his head is juggling what appears to be his own bloody eyeballs. Straight ahead, a disheveled woman dragging a heavy burlap sack behind her cackles as she weaves in and out of the food truck lines.

When he reaches the ticket trailer at the edge of the grassy plaza, a woman with a pink mohawk glances up at him for a fraction of a second. Then she averts her eyes and reaches out to take a handful of bills. She doesn't wave in greeting, and he doesn't acknowledge her either. Staff members aren't supposed to interact with each other in any way that might break the spell.

Not in front of guests.

On a whim, he steps into the yellow circle cast by the streetlight directly above the ticket trailer, then turns back toward the dark plaza.

Behind the mask, he smiles. And waves.

The first five rows of the unlit parking lot—which isn't so much a parking lot as it is a long field that has been mowed over to allow for parking—are packed with cars. Still, the lot is maybe a tenth full. In October, all of the rows will be packed.

A steady stream of blinding headlights and glowing red taillights will snake through the reflective rope switchbacks that lead to and from the Thicket exit.

His car is tucked into the darkness at the very edge of the lot, where the scrubby cut grass and leveled dirt give way to cornfields. The breeze is picking up now, rattling the half-dry stalks in a soft, papery patter.

He opens the driver's side and stands in the spiky grass while he removes the mask, his shoes, and his clothing down to his underwear. He carefully places the knife and mask on a tarp laid across the passenger seat and nestles the pile of dirty clothing on top. Then he pulls on a fresh pair of sweats and a hoodie from a backpack in the backseat.

As he eases into the driver's side, he wonders how long it will be before they find the bodies.

And how long it will be before the trickle of thrill-seekers realize that they brushed past the real thing.

CHAPTER 8

Norah registers the sirens in the distance as she scrolls through her Facebook feed. But it isn't until she looks up to see the woman with the pink mohawk—the one who was taking tickets earlier—walking toward her that she knows in her gut something very bad has happened.

The screams that have become part of the rise and fall of the background chaos in the Thicket feel like a chorus as the woman with the pink hair takes Norah by the hand. She squeezes it hard and says, "I need you to come with me, sweetie." Then she leads the way toward the trailer.

Around them, the food stalls are rapidly closing down. And scarers cloaked in fur, blood, and latex masks begin to herd confused teens toward the exits. Norah doesn't ask why. Because the look in the woman's eyes tells her to cling to these last few minutes of not-knowing like a life raft.

CHAPTER 9

He keeps the TV on Channel Two while he stands, stripped down to his underwear, in front of the washing machine. He slowly adds the baking soda, then another bottle of spray-and-wash.

He should get into the shower, but he doesn't want to miss anything when the story breaks.

He waits another thirty minutes. An hour.

Just as he turns on the water to the shower, he hears the anchor say, ". . . breaking live at the Thicket . . ."

He turns the stream of hot water off.

A reporter is standing near the ticket trailer at the Thicket, gesturing to the empty plaza.

Red and blue police lights fill the scene as the woman tells Channel Two what she knows.

Two dead.

Multiple stab wounds.

Heinous crime. Brutal murders. Premeditated.

The Thicket has already made an official statement, expressing their outrage and deep condolences to the families of the victims—and pledging metal detectors and better security.

The reporter promises to share all new developments as they emerge.

There are no leads.

CHAPTER 10

October 1st

The trampoline sways up and down while Jamie talks, motioning with her hands. Her long auburn hair flies across her shoulders in soft waves as she bounces. Taylor closes her eyes and smiles, content to let Jamie go on.

Somewhere nearby, one of the neighbors is grilling hot dogs. The sweet, charred smell mingles with something earthy and overripe from the garden a few feet away. In the newly crimson hedges that form a line in front of the old wood fence, the first crickets are already singing. The crickets' chirps stall and start as Jamie's high, fast voice cuts through the stillness of the cool evening air. "He's totally not as cute as he thinks he is either," she's saying. "Annie said she saw him in, like, a Speedo in middle school, and . . ."

Taylor lets her mind drift, wondering how cold it's going to get tonight. It's not even really jacket weather yet—not during the day, anyway. "Indian summer," her dad keeps repeating, peering through the kitchen window at the garden boxes still loaded with red and green tomatoes. Still, the air has a familiar bite to it, and Taylor has a feeling that she, Maren, and Jamie will be piled on Jamie's living room floor by morning. Like always.

Opening her eyes a slit, Taylor can just see a swath of neon light blinking from inside the house. In the living room, Jamie's mom is a dark silhouette on the worn corduroy loveseat, glued to the TV. Snatches of indistinguishable rapid-fire banter between anchors drift through the open screen door a few yards away.

To Taylor's right, Maren burrows deeper into her nest of sleeping bags and lumped-up pillows. When Jamie doesn't even pause in her rant, Maren sighs loudly and pulls a blanket up over her face, leaving just a shock of short blond hair visible at the top of her purple pillow. Taylor stifles a laugh. Maren has been itching to interrupt Jamie, who has been ticking off an exhaustive list of Russ Nielsen's flaws for at least fifteen minutes.

There's an unspoken understanding that Jamie actually wants Russ to ask her to homecoming.

"He wears the same shirt every three days. And he bugs me for a pen in pre-calc like, *every single day.* Like, how is he going through *that many pens?* And why is he using a freakin' pen to do math anyway? You're supposed to use a pencil."

The trampoline bows, then bucks, as Jamie throws her hands out in front of her in exasperation. She snatches at a long lock of ginger hair and begins picking at the strands.

Taylor closes her eyes and smiles.

Maren sighs heavily again, louder this time. "The shirt thing is normal. Boys do that. My dad *still* does that. And maybe he's writing you a note. A really long note. To . . . ask you to homecoming."

Jamie huffs, her voice rising another octave. "The dance is in like, two weeks. *Two weeks.* If he wanted to ask me, he should have done it by now. Everything is already picked over. I'll have to shop at, like, the Dress Barn."

Maren moans underneath the blanket, and Taylor can almost feel the eye roll. "Well, shit. Jamie might have to shop at Dress Barn. Do you guys still want to order pizza? I'm starving. Taylor? *Please* don't tell me you're asleep already over there."

Taylor opens her eyes and smiles, sitting up a little in the sleeping bag and pulling the blanket off Maren's face. "I definitely want pizza. James, how about you?"

Jamie frowns and flops onto her stomach, burying her head into a mound of blankets. Her hair cascades around her in a way that makes Taylor think of *The Little Mermaid* and consider dying her own hair that shade of red. "I don't even care."

Maren shoots Taylor a look that says, *It's your turn to save this sleepover.*

Taylor considers her options. Then she bounces once and gently flings herself on top of Jamie, who lets out a squeak. "Come *on,* James. Your neighbor is over there grilling like, 500 hot dogs. There is actual drool on my pillow. I ate dinner at 4:30, which means it basically counted as a second lunch. I'm *starving.*"

She bounces a little more, and Jamie starts to laugh, the sound pealing through the backyard like bell chimes. "Okay, fine, fine, stop." She pushes herself upright. "You're going to make me pee my freakin' pants. Screw Russ. Let's go order pizza."

As they troop back to the house, Taylor hears voices rising above the drone of the TV. Jamie's dad must have gotten home.

"Well, *I* signed the petition," Jamie's mom is saying, her voice strained. "What happened was just an accident waiting to happen, if you ask me. And it could happen again. I don't understand what's so crazy about taking precautions."

Jamie's dad snorts. "Accident, my ass. That guy knew exactly what he was doing. Bad things happen, and you can't stop them by turning the whole world into a padded room. What about the shootings at the post office? Let's close that down too. *That* place is an accident waiting to happen."

Jamie reaches for the screen door and shakes her head slightly, nodding toward the dark hallway that leads to her bedroom. Everyone's parents and neighbors and PTAs are saying the same thing. *Shut it down.*

The online petition for a shutdown started circulating the day after the murders, following an interview with Norah's mother—Brandon's mother—on KQRZ. The petition has gotten more than 100,000 signatures so far. Not all of them from Southeast Idaho, either.

Taylor has agonized over whether she should reach out to Norah—who hasn't been at school for a week—over Facebook. But it's not like they know each other. Not really. Not anymore.

Taylor, Norah, Maren, and Jamie were in the same homeroom in middle school. But freshman year sifted them into different classes, different groups. Taylor, Maren, and Jamie took choir and attended National Honor Society meetings over lunch. Norah started wearing thick black eyeliner and got busted for smoking in the photography room.

"Hey, girls!" Jamie's mom puts on a smile and pats the empty couch cushion beside her as she notices Jamie. She's sitting with a glass of water clutched in one hand, the TV remote in the other, staring at the TV screen.

Jamie's dad, who looks tired and cranky, rubs the week's worth of stubble on his chin. As Taylor waves awkwardly, he mumbles a hello then retreats through the kitchen toward the garage.

On Channel Two, a woman with a short blond bob cut is standing in front of the ticket trailer at the Thicket, gesturing to a tech in scrubs. The tech is walking away quickly in the other direction, his face obscured by a blue paper mask.

". . . Thicket announced that pathologists have completed their initial investigation. Degrading and contaminated evidence from the initial crime scene has created a nightmare situation for investigators and forensic specialists."

"Hey, Mom," Jamie says with a sigh and walks toward the couch.

"Hi, Mrs. Edwards," Maren and Taylor say in unison, hanging back at the kitchen table.

Jamie's mom looks like she is about to say something lighthearted, her mouth half-turned into a smile. But then the anchor with the blond hair starts talking over B-roll from opening weekend at the Thicket, and everyone leans in to listen. It's impossible to look away.

"The Thicket is as old as Declo itself. The twenty cabins that dot the infamous wooded trails—along with a bunkhouse, school, mess hall, mill, and laundry facilities—were originally built in 1923 for the families of field hands and factory workers employed by Wind River Sugar Factory.

"After World War II, when most of Wind River's staff went off to war, the outdated cabins sat empty. In the 70s, an investor purchased the land and wired the buildings for electricity, with the intent of renting them out for family reunions. However, the history of accidental deaths among the field workers who lived in the cabins, along with the remote location, drove him out of business."

B-roll of the original cabins in various states of disrepair flashes across the screen. "The land sat vacant again, a magnet for graffiti, vagrants, and even rumors of occult worship. Then, in the mid-90s, a second investor purchased the wooded portion of the land and turned it into the Thicket we now know, complete with a corn maze leased from Wind River."

The news anchor smiles as if revealing a particularly important plot twist. "This time, the ancient cabins, graffiti, and rumors of occult worship became assets. The new haunted attraction brought a steady stream of thrill-seekers to Declo each Halloween to explore the forest trails and enjoy the festivities in the plaza, the site of the original mess hall for Wind River employees."

The anchor continues. "But the massive attraction that draws thousands from the pacific northwest didn't come into its own until five years ago, when a prop malfunction resulted in the death of a staff member. That accident nearly closed the operation for good. Traffic dwindled, and an undisclosed settlement was paid to the victim's family members.

Taylor has actually heard this part of the story before but assumed it was a rumor. She glances sideways at Jamie and Maren, who are now watching the TV in earnest, transfixed. Jamie's feet are tucked against her mom's, and Taylor feels a pang of jealousy.

"Despite the financial blow—and the tragedy itself—the incident is widely considered to be the cause of the Thicket's massive growth and success. In 2012, the TV series *Ghost Hunters* featured the Thicket in an episode, using so-called 'spirit boxes,' and heat sensors to capture paranormal activity. The crew spent a night in the old mill to 'commune' with the staff member who had died in the accident.

"When the episode aired, *Ghost Hunters* purported that the Thicket was indeed haunted by the spirits of numerous factory workers, including the spirit of the staff member. The episode effectively put Declo, Idaho, on the map for every Halloween enthusiast in the Pacific Northwest. Since then, the Thicket has completed a massive renovation and expansion of the plaza, added concession stands, a DJ, and increasingly elaborate props and effects, earning it the honor of 'Top 10 haunted houses in the US' every year since."

A new image appears on screen, an old map of the Thicket with a thin black *X* drawn over a section near the top of the map. The anchor says, "In response to public outcry and widespread petitions after the prop malfunction death, ten acres of the original Thicket, including the old mill, were closed to the public. Now, five years later, the Thicket once again finds itself in the crosshairs of public outcry and calls for a shutdown on the heels of the most recent tragedy. Still, some thrill-seekers have once again countered the petitions for a shutdown with petitions to keep the Thicket open."

At the mention of the counter-petitions, Taylor feels Maren shift a little beside her. Jamie's mom frowns, and for a second Taylor is afraid she's going to ask about the petitions.

Taking the cue to leave, Jamie stands up and motions toward the bedroom again. "We're going to order pizza, okay, Mom?"

Most of the counter-petitions have been started by students at local middle and high schools. Maren has started the one at Centennial—but nobody is supposed to know that. Especially not Jamie's mom, who is gathering signatures for the shut-it-down side.

For the past two weeks, the Thicket's fate has remained uncertain, the entire operation surrounded by caution tape, police cars, white vans, and a thick sea of onlookers from the county highway. Taylor reluctantly signed Maren's petition after Maren swore up and down that the only people who would ever see it would be management at the Thicket. No teachers—and god forbid not Norah or her family.

Jamie's mom lifts the remote and changes the channel as Jamie retreats. An elderly woman with a tight gray bun appears on screen, holding up one corner of a red-and-pink patchwork quilt to the camera.

"Sorry, girls. I know hearing about this awful situation nonstop must be so stressful for you. It's giving me nightmares, but I can't stop watching it."

Maren and Taylor exchange glances. "It's okay. You can turn it back on," Maren says. "I heard they're doing a feature about the creepy mask he was wearing later; you should keep watching."

Jamie's mom blinks. "What do you mean?"

Jamie, who has almost disappeared down the hallway to her bedroom, turns around. She shoots Maren an exasperated look. *Shut up,* she mouths. Then she calls, "Nothing, Mom," and disappears down the hall.

Maren pauses, tucking a few wispy strands of blond hair behind her ears. "So, someone found the exact same mask that guy wore, and started selling them on eBay—"

Jamie sighs as she reappears from the hallway. "It's just another story, Mom. Like, don't even watch it. Nobody at Centennial has one of those masks." From behind the wall, where her mom can't see it, Jamie flips her middle finger at Maren.

Maren grins wickedly.

The masks were officially banned from the high school grounds that afternoon. And Taylor knows of at least two kids in her homeroom who have purchased one online. But details.

Jamie's mom purses her lips and frowns at the woman on the TV, who is pointing at the quilt's piping. "I can't help it. All of this just hits so close to home. Those poor parents. I just can't even imagine what they're going through. Why would anyone want one of those masks?"

Jamie motions for Taylor and Maren to follow her down the hallway. "You should stick with PBS for a while, Mom," she calls again, turning back around and heading for her bedroom. "Take a break."

Jamie's mom sighs and turns back to the TV, watching the woman with the quilt for a few moments before flipping back to the news as she settles into the loveseat.

CHAPTER 11

His mind wanders through the segment about the Thicket's history and a jarring commercial break.

But when the footage changes to an aerial view of the Thicket, he moves closer to the TV.

The camera in the helicopter zooms in on the dusky gray horizon beyond the corn maze, showing the black outline of a rooftop beyond the endless sea of waving stalks.

As the camera pans across the black rooftop, bringing the building into better focus, the blond anchor—Caroline—sums up the story of the old gallows malfunction. The incident happened five years earlier in the old mill. It nearly closed the entire operation down.

Unconsciously, he lifts a finger to his mouth and tastes the faint, metallic tang of blood.

He can still remember the feel of the lumpy sawdust beneath his feet in the old mill. And the heft of the rope in his hands. Coarse, thick, substantial, and unyielding.

He can still hear the onlookers' incredulous gasps as the trapdoor above the corn sifter released with a hollow-sounding thunk, sending the redheaded boy swinging through the opening below, screaming and struggling as the rope appeared to pull taut against his neck.

The gallows illusion had been brilliant, hinging on a strand of razor-thin piano wire that snapped and hummed as it went taut, catching the boy safely as he fell. The piano wire was invisible to the audience, who saw a hanged man sway limply back and forth from the visible but impotent rope.

The gallows trick was an audience favorite.

Tim was the star of the show.

Until that night.

The story was all over the news five years ago. The death had quickly been ruled an accident, but the old mill and gallows act were no longer included in the Thicket. That section of trail had been permanently closed.

He remembers how the policewoman touched his arm lightly while he told her what had happened, tears pooling in his eyes and snot running down his nose. "The wire just . . . it just snapped, I guess. I really thought it was all part of the act. Just like everyone else. We'd done it hundreds of times before. Tim was such a good actor. I had no idea. By the time I realized . . ."

He'd been asked to work Concessions in the plaza for the rest of that season, scooping an endless stream of donuts out of hot, amber grease.

"We want you to know that we don't blame you for what happened," his supervisor, a woman with short, brown hair and wide hazel eyes, said. "Our lawyers actually advised us to let you go. But we felt that was excessive. This is our compromise."

He hadn't been hired back for the following season. Or the season after that.

It had been a disappointment at the time. But he didn't mind anymore.

Things had a way of working out.

CHAPTER 12

"We've got almost 500 signatures," Maren whispers as Jamie shuts the door to her bedroom and locks it.

Taylor grins and flops down on the bed. From what her dad said, none of the petitions had any real legal clout to shut the Thicket down. The families would have to file an official suit against the haunted attraction, which could take months if not years. In other words, the petitions were mostly useless, and nobody at Centennial High School had a real say in the outcome.

Taylor figures her dad is right. He is an attorney. But still.

"How many more signatures are you trying to get? Jamie asks. Then, without waiting for an answer, she whispers, "You guys, Russ's friend totally got one."

"A petition?" Maren asks, confused. "I'm already—"

"No, one of those masks." Jamie giggles. "He had it in his backpack today. He's going to wear it to Maisie's party."

Taylor wraps her arms around her stomach and sits next to Maren on the daybed. Through the wall to the living room, she can hear the sound of the news anchors talking again. "Yeah. Maisie Barrett got one too. She put it on while Mrs. Jackman went to the bathroom during first period. Did . . . did you see the news story yesterday? With uh, Mrs. Lewis?" When Maren looks confused Taylor adds, "You know. Norah's mom."

Jamie looks up from her phone and wrinkles her nose. "No. What did she say?"

Maren pulls a pillow to her chest and unlocks her phone with a quiet *click*. "I saw part of it. It was *super* sad. They asked her about the masks—and the petitions—and she just freaking *lost* it. Total mental breakdown on camera. Ugly crying and everything." Maren scrolls through the photos in her iPhone and holds it out so Taylor can see. "Oh! And have you seen this shit? It's so messed up. My sister sent it—"

Taylor squeezes her eyes shut tightly as her stomach rolls. "No! I . . . I accidentally saw those photos a few days ago. I can't look at them again."

Brandon Lewis had texted three images the night he was murdered. He sent them to the three boys who were supposed to go with him to the Thicket. A bloody cow eye, a woman with an ax in her back—and a corpse in a bathtub filled with blood.

The last one, of course, had been real. The staff member's face had been covered with blood. Real blood. Taylor still sees it when she's trying to fall asleep at night. The photos were leaked right after the news story broke. At first, there were rumors that Brandon had been trying to give police some kind of message about the person who had killed him. But from the police's carefully worded statement, it sounded like he was just impressed with the Thicket's effects.

Taylor hopes Norah hasn't seen the photos. Her Facebook profile is still nowhere to be seen. But the photos have been everywhere.

"No, silly. Not *those* photos," Maren chides, nudging Taylor with the phone. "Look. Some dorks made his locker into, like, a freaking shrine." She zooms in on the lower right corner of one photo, shaking her head. "Look at that one, with all the hearts and sad faces. My sister says he was actually kind of a dick. Do you remember the one time we went to Norah's house and he asked Jamie about her *bra size—*"

"Maren!" Jamie squeaks and throws one of the pillows from the futon near the door.

The pillow bounces off the side of the bed. Maren pulls up her feet and laughs, her fine, white-blond hair floating around her cheeks like dandelion down. "What? It sucks, but dying doesn't turn him into an angel."

Taylor sighs and sinks back into the pillows on the daybed, relieved that it's just a photo of some flowers and notes on Brandon's locker. "Have either of you heard anything from Norah?" she asks tentatively.

Maren turns and raises an eyebrow. "No, have you? I can't remember the last time I talked to her. Like, I feel bad for her. But I'm not making shrines or anything."

Jamie shrugs in agreement, and Taylor feels her cheeks turning pink. "Yeah, totally. I just hope she's okay. Hey, can we *please* order the pizza now? And can we *please* get a vegetarian this time? Maisie told me how they make pepperoni, and now I can't even."

Jamie holds up her phone triumphantly. "I already ordered. One veggie, one pepperoni. *All* the pizzas. You're welcome." She makes a little bow on the edge of the futon then jumps onto the bed between Taylor and Maren. She lays her head on Maren's leg and looks at Taylor. "Truth or truth?"

Taylor laughs, tugging her hair out of a ponytail to start a thick braid. "Uh, truth, I guess." She glances between Jamie and Maren as she pretends to think, then laughs. "Hold on— no—*truth.*"

They'd long since run out of ideas for the "dare" part of truth-or-dare. Dares were really only fun when they involved boys, anyway.

Jamie nods, her pale blue eyes serious. "Maren?"

Maren picks at a piece of lint on her fleece hoodie and shrugs. "Fine, truth."

"If the Thicket reopens, are we going?"

Maren flicks a piece of lint at Jamie, who squeals. "It's definitely going to reopen," she says. "You heard what they said on the news about the rope accident where the guy died in the mill. My mom said it almost closed back then—for good. But it just made the place more popular."

Jamie nods thoughtfully. "Okay, so you'd go?"

Maren sighs loudly but can't keep from smiling. "God, I'm hungry. And yes, obviously I'd go. I started the petition, didn't I?" She glances toward the door and fluffs up the back of her short hair. "Tay?"

It's been a few years since Taylor has been to the Thicket. It's a forty-five-minute drive from Rupert to Declo on bad roads. She remembers begging her dad to go with Jamie and Maren when she was thirteen. Maren had to be escorted out of the Thicket by a staff member that first year—a fact she denies point-blank to this day. But with the Thicket in nonstop local features that are getting picked up by outlets across the US, it's all anyone at Centennial High School is talking about. Taylor nods slowly. "Yeah, I'd go. It's probably safer now than it was before. Would you, James?"

The doorbell rings and Jamie jumps to her feet with a grin, knocking half the pillows off the bed. "Yes and yes. Come on, let's take the pizza back out to the trampoline." She motions toward a white air return just visible behind the daybed then lowers her voice. "My mom's probably listening at the vent anyway."

* * *

By the time both pizza boxes are empty, the chill in the night air is sharper. Inside, Jamie's mom has turned off the TV and gone to bed, leaving the house still and dark. Taylor snuggles deeper into her sleeping bag on the trampoline and zips it up to her chin.

The brittle black leaves from the sycamore tree overhead rustle quietly, hiding and then revealing stars. Every few seconds, another leaf flutters slowly onto the growing pile on the trampoline.

"I'm so full I can't even breathe," Jamie whispers from inside her sleeping bag. "Did anyone else besides me even eat the pepperoni one?"

"I had at least three pieces of both," Maren giggles back, burrowing deeper beneath her blanket. "Good thing we're sleeping outside tonight."

"Gross," Jamie squeals, poking her head back out of the mound of blankets and shifting away from Maren. "You're sleeping on that side of the tramp."

A twig snaps from somewhere in the neighboring yard. Taylor eases out of her sleeping bag and whispers, "What if he's over there now, standing behind that fence?" She nods toward the warped wood slats a few feet away, looming black above the dull red of the bushes.

"Oh, he's totally out there," Jamie says seriously. She pauses, then adds, "Jim, my neighbor that is. He wears these weird little man-shorts when he mows the lawn. He's probably raking leaves in them right now."

Taylor giggles. "Ew. You know who I mean. The guy from the Thicket. Norah's family lives, like, five minutes from here. What if the guy's been in your neighborhood? "

There is a scurrying sound, followed by a loud slam against the side of the fence.

Maren shrieks and catapults out of her sleeping bag, flinging her legs over the side of the trampoline to run. Taylor freezes.

Jamie sucks in her breath then starts to laugh, scooping up a handful of leaves that have accumulated on top of her sleeping bag and tossing them at the fence. "Calm down, you guys. It's just Pete."

At the top of the fence, eyes glowing green, is Pete. Jamie's enormous orange cat, returning from the neighbor's yard.

Maren stands barefoot in the middle of the lawn, her black-lined, green eyes wide in the dark. Her sleeping bag dangles halfway off the trampoline. She lets out a sigh of relief but shakes her head. "*Shit.* Can we actually go back inside? He really *is* out there somewhere."

Jamie makes a knowing *mm hmm* sound, but Taylor starts to gather up her sleeping bag. "We end up inside every time anyway, James. Plus, I already have to pee again. Come on, let's go inside."

CHAPTER 13

At nine o'clock, the Channel Two logo flashes across the silent, flickering TV screen. The camera pans around the studio and rests on the woman anchor with the wispy bob haircut.

He turns up the volume on the TV.

"Thanks for joining us. I'm Caroline Tolley, and this is Gary Lebhart," the woman says. The camera angles wide to show a thickset, smiling man with a close-cropped brown mustache beside her.

He watches eagerly as Caroline announces the top story. As usual, it's the Thicket.

The networks can't help playing the same five seconds of security footage in slow motion every time a news segment runs. The clip is online, too. One video on Youtube has eighteen million views and counting.

It never gets old. As Caroline talks, he watches himself walk through the middle of the plaza, at 8:00 pm on a Tuesday. The grainy image shows kids laughing and sidestepping to let him pass through the lines near the food trucks. Some don't even look at him. You can even see a security guard in one frame for a split second.

At the end of the recording, he steps into the light near the ticket trailer, looks up at the camera, and waves. Then he disappears into the parking lot.

The image on screen changes to a freeze-frame of his hand lifted mid-wave. Leaning forward on the couch, he mimes the wave.

When the two anchors reappear on screen, Caroline Tolley's lips are set in a terse, straight line.

He watches the muscle in her jaw tighten as she reminds viewers that there is still no determination as to whether the Thicket will be reopening.

Caroline doesn't like to give him the spotlight. He can tell by the way her thin upper lip curls to the right whenever she's forced to mention "the perpetrator," as she always calls him. So clinical. So impersonal.

Still, Channel Two is what he watches most. He likes to see Caroline squirm through these news stories. He almost wishes she knew his name so he could watch her say it.

But Gary is already moving on to the weather. The usual bait-and-switch. Lead with the juicy stuff. Sneak in the weather and a local feel-good piece about someone rescuing a three-legged dog from a storm drain. Tease the big breaking story again. Then, finally, as the big hand on the clock starts its upward swing to close the hour, it'll be time to dive back into the real story. The only reason anyone is watching Channel Two tonight.

He understands the technique. It's all about building anticipation.

Gary the weather forecaster goes on about dropping temperatures and cold snaps—*get those tomatoes covered, folks!*

Restless, he turns away from the TV and yawns. On the coffee table near his legs, a fly is crawling across the shiny wood surface.

He studies it for a moment. It hops once, then twice, then continues inching toward the edge. It doesn't appear to be able to fly.

He leans over, bringing his face close enough to the table that he can see the fly's spiky legs rubbing together in front of its face in quick, hair-trigger motions.

Then he reaches out a hand and covers the insect gently, feeling it pinball back and forth across his palm, buzzing violently then quieting.

Cupping his other hand beneath it at the edge of the coffee table, he pinches the fly between two fingers. Then deftly removes both wings. Followed by the legs.

When he's done, he sets the tiny black lump on the edge of the recliner, careful not to tip it off onto the brown shag carpet.

The fly is quiet now.

He watches it long after the 9:00 news has ended and the theme music to "Seinfeld" begins to blare from the small TV.

The two red, twitching eyes are the only indication that it's still alive.

CHAPTER 14

When the sound of voices drifts through the still-dark house, Taylor rolls over sleepily and pulls Jamie's pink duvet underneath her chin.

It's early, she gauges by the gray light coming through the blinds. Can't be much after seven. Jamie is still curled up on the futon across the room, one side of her sleeping bag splayed open to show her fleece panda pajamas.

On the other side of the bed next to Taylor, Maren is still snoring softly, her short blond hair draped over one eye.

Sitting up and scooting to the foot of the bed, Taylor listens at the door crack as the drifting voices rise and fall.

"So you'd let Jamie go? Is that what you're saying?" It's Jamie's mom.

". . . Kris. She's sixteen. We can't keep her in a bubble," says Jamie's dad. Taylor strains to hear as his voice drifts away.

"This isn't a bubble, David. They're opening up a *week* after two closed-casket funerals. The Lewises live just a few blocks away," Jamie's mom says a little louder.

Taylor is fully awake now. She turns and shakes Maren's shoulder, then quietly gets out of bed and pads across the carpet to wake Jamie. "Wake up, you guys. *Shh.* I think something happened."

Jamie groggily rolls off the futon and motions to the daybed. Then she carefully lifts one corner of the bed frame to pull it away from the wall. "Come on. The vent listening goes both ways."

Giggling softly, Jamie and Taylor slide between the wall and the bed on one side, crouching beside the vent. Maren army crawls down the narrow strip of carpet beneath the bed.

The TV is on again—the news. And through the vent, they can hear it almost as well as if they were standing in the living room with Jamie's parents.

". . . assured patrons that this was a tragic but isolated incident, and that the Thicket will continue working closely with police and authorities to establish the facts around the two slayings. But at this time, as the official crime scene processing concludes, we have learned that the Thicket will be reopened with additional security and safety precautions."

Maren's eyes widen, and she slaps at Jamie's arm in excitement. "Shh!" Taylor whispers, dying to hear the rest.

A woman with a brusque voice is speaking now. "Our hearts go out to these families. Safety is our number-one concern, and we will work tirelessly to ensure that all guests have a safe and enjoyable experience at the Thicket."

As the male news anchor takes over again, repeating what he just said about the Thicket reopening on Monday, Jamie's parents begin arguing where they left off.

Maren pokes at Jamie's arm again from under the bed then reaches up to shake Taylor's shoulder. "Truth or truth—final answer, bitches," she whispers excitedly. "Are we going to the Thicket this year?"

Jamie scrunches up her nose and pulls at a few tangles in her thick auburn hair. She carefully extricates herself from the space between the wall and the bed then shrugs. "My mom will kill me if a random psychopath doesn't. But I'm in."

Taylor grins and decides she is definitely dying her hair red. "I'm in too."

CHAPTER 15

October 4th

Norah mutes the TV as the anchors exclaim over the big news.

It's already all over the Internet. The story broke early this morning.

The Thicket is reopening.

Norah stares at the small TV in the dimly lit living room and tries to find the rage she felt earlier this morning. But she can't seem to find it. The white-hot anger broke the surface then disappeared into a sea of nothingness. The counselor she saw last week says that's normal. Which seems like a strange way to put things.

The anchors on screen gesture animatedly. The dark-haired weather reporter, Gary, grimaces and shakes his head. The blond woman with the pristinely highlighted bob purses her lips and frowns. The banner running beneath them on the screen reads, "Thicket Reopens After Double Slaying Despite Protests."

Norah watches the silent TV in her silent house until she sees her own living room reflected back at her. Then she grabs the remote to turn the volume back on. Her mom did an interview with Channel Two last night at the house, after the press conference. Her mom, who is still asleep upstairs and doesn't yet know about the Thicket's reopening.

The house looks terrible, Norah notices as the camera view changes and she stares at her own messy living room on the

TV screen. The field reporter is perched on the very edge of the sofa while he talks to Norah's mom. It's hard to tell if his rear end is even touching the cushion. It's probably for the best, since there are two very greasy paper plates in the middle of the couch.

Norah glances to her left. The greasy paper plates are still there. The house hasn't been cleaned for almost a month.

Norah leaves the plates where they are, but as she pulls her cold toes up beneath her on the sofa, she nudges a fun-size Twix wrapper onto the carpet. A few flakes of chocolate spill onto the already dingy cream shag rug.

Norah's stomach clenches as she watches her mom make the latest stuttering, incoherent plea for viewers to step forward with new information. Her mom's voice sounds thin and wavering. Like she's asking for a personal and unlikely favor. Her chin is quivering so hard that she can't get some of the words out fully.

Norah feels a muted wave of nausea.

The field reporter nods sympathetically and ends the interview. *Back to you, Gary and Carol.*

Back in the blue-lit studio, the anchors shake their heads. *Poor family. So very difficult. Hope they catch this guy soon.* Then Gary repeats the salient details of the breaking story: the Thicket is reopening.

Norah lays down on the couch next to the greasy plates and listens to Gary share the same information about the reopening. She reaches for the Twix wrapper lying on the rug. She knows she didn't eat the piece of candy. And it wasn't her dad, who insists chocolate tastes like vomit. Or her mom, who hasn't really eaten anything over the past month.

Which leaves Brandon.

Norah crumples the metallic wrapper into her palm, rolling the foil tight until the inside of her knuckles starts to hurt. But after a few minutes, even they go numb.

Yesterday while Channel Two interviewed her mom, Norah stayed upstairs. From her bedroom window, she watched the field reporter load his camera into the van with the tall blue "Eyewitness Channel Two" in vinyl letters on the side. A group of kids across the street were standing in a driveway a few houses down, watching too.

They were Brandon's age. Middle school. Two boys and a girl. Norah didn't recognize them. All three were crowded on the edge of a dented green transformer, shoulders touching. They were watching the news van with unabashed, wide-eyed interest.

The only thing missing was the popcorn.

Norah had opened the window carefully, deciding to eavesdrop, although with the wind in the aspens out front, she couldn't hear much.

One of the kids—a boy with a blue flannel shirt—pointed at Norah's front door. Then he grabbed the girl's shoulders playfully with one hand while making a stabbing motion with the other. The girl flipped him off as she jumped off the edge of the transformer. It wasn't hard to catch the gist of what they were saying.

Norah had shut the window, and put her headphones in, no longer wanting to hear what was being said outside or downstairs in her living room. As The Smiths sang about Lesly Ann being buried on the moors, she closed her eyes and tried to drift away. When she couldn't, she popped a blackberry pot gummy into her mouth and imagined herself confronting the boy with the flannel shirt. She is pretty sure she could make him cry.

Sad. Bitch be crazy, Norah thinks about herself. That's what Blink2002 had posted to the comments section of an online clip of Norah's mom. The clip showed Mrs. Lewis leaving the podium mid-sentence, weeping, at Friday's police press conference.

Another comment, this one from BroncoBrony, said, *This kid was like, 12. Right? Who just dumped him off at the Thicket alone, anyway?*

Blink2002 and BroncoBrony made good points.

The clip of the press conference had 2 million views already. More people than there were in the entire state of Idaho. And it wasn't the only thing making the rounds on social media.

Channel Two had interviewed Brandon's friends last week. *Friends.*

They'd admitted to standing him up the night he was murdered. Cole. And Jace. And Andrew. "We'd never planned on meeting him at the Thicket," they'd said. "We were just joking around with him. He wasn't really in our group. He was . . . you know . . . on the spectrum or something. We all feel really bad now after, you know . . ."

That video had 4.3 million views.

Brandon had been talking about all three boys since the start of the school year. He had started wearing Gap jeans because Jace had them. And he'd started leaving his laces undone because Cole did.

None of the boys had ever been to Brandon's house. Last week, Norah had used a fake Facebook account to comment on the interview with Cole, Jace, and Andrew. *Who needs enemies with shithead friends like you?* she'd typed, clinging to the white-hot anger until it slipped back beneath the surface.

A few days later, Norah saw that Jace had posted a public photo on his Facebook wall of flowers and notes taped to Brandon's locker at the middle school. "RIP, buddy," it said. Norah had logged into her fake account to comment on that post, too. The comment had been quickly deleted.

Norah's attention drifts back to the news report. "A statement released by the principal at Minico Middle revealed that the school will join other local schools in banning the so-called 'plague doctor' masks on school grounds. . ."

Norah feels the bile rise in her throat. *Plague doctor.* Sometimes the name drifts into her consciousness as she tries to fall asleep. The words circle like smoke, threatening to seep into her dreams. And often they do.

Caroline acknowledges a man in a tweed jacket who has just appeared in the upper corner of the news screen. "Thanks for joining us, Professor Mickelson. Can you tell us what a 'plague doctor' is?"

The professor smiles. "Certainly. In the 17th century 'plague doctors,' were commonly retained by cities or municipalities to treat victims of the bubonic plague. Most plague doctors were not professionally trained physicians but rather young, unestablished, or opportunistic lay citizens. Most wore a waxed overcoat to repel any inadvertent contact with bodily fluids and a beak-like mask filled with aromatics, flowers, and oils to filter the smell of death and infection.

"Plague doctors used 'bloodletting' as a primary 'cure,' a practice that often resulted in the death of the patient and in spreading the plague. In general, plague doctors were kept isolated from the public due to the nature of their craft. Unlike most doctors at the time, plague doctors were often authorized to conduct autopsies."

Bloodletting. Norah swallows back the bile and sits up on the couch. The sound of the newscasters' voices in the background blend together in a dull roar.

SocialBuzz featured a beaked black look-alike mask three days after the national news channels started airing the story and playing the security footage. The article shared the gruesome histories of some of the most famous plague doctors in the middle ages, along with a link to buy the exact mask used in the "plague doctor murders."

After the predictable backlash on Twitter, the link in the article was removed. But not before the mask went viral in Southeast Idaho and beyond.

Norah finally turns off the TV and waits until she is sure she won't throw up. The living room is so quiet she can hear the fizz of the aquarium filter in the corner, near the kitchen. A lone goldfish hovers near the top, circling the tank in a slow lap. She wonders if her dad has been feeding it. She certainly hasn't.

Norah's not sure where her dad is now. His car isn't in the driveway. He seems to have stopped sleeping in direct proportion to how seldom Norah's mom gets out of bed. As to balance the universe, maybe.

Norah watches the goldfish's mouth open and close as the little orange creature shimmies near the surface. Waiting for someone to finally open the dusty lid to sprinkle a few fish flakes.

As Norah heads upstairs, she imagines walking by the tank in the morning to find the fish dead.

It would be her fault, of course.

CHAPTER 16

The Channel Two jingle plays with a frenetic burst of jazzy elevator music after the commercial break. He leans closer to the screen, bringing one hand to his mouth to suck on the tip of his pointer finger as he settles back against the couch.

The TV has been on for days now. Each news segment, no matter how repetitive, is another small shot of adrenaline.

As the two anchors reappear on screen, Caroline Tolley states—again—that the Thicket has announced its plans to reopen this coming Monday Her jaw tightens as she says the words.

He can see the flash of relief on her face when the weather forecaster takes over to drone on about a chance of snow in the forecast—*get that ice melt ready!*

Satisfied for the moment, he stretches and walks to his bedroom. The mask is in his bottom drawer, covered by an assortment of black socks and white briefs that could use a good bleaching.

The copycat "plague-doctor" masks are spreading like wildfire. A couple of the masks have even appeared in the community Buy-N-Sell group he's a member of on Facebook, to the anguish of local parents. All of this makes him feel better about keeping the original. The clown mask, on the other hand, is safely buried in the dump by now. The soft, tufted red hair on the sides concerned him. Porous things were more dangerous than rubber or metal.

He takes the mask with him into the living room and holds the thin latex up to his nose. The acrid rubber is now squeaky clean, but it still evokes the memory of blood.

As Gary yammers on about something weather-related and inconsequential, he wriggles his fingers through the dark eyeholes of the mask. In and out, like thin white worms.

He remembers the flash of outrage on the staff member's maskless, acne-covered face. And the way that outrage suddenly evaporated when the knife appeared.

He remembers the way the second kid's eyes widened. And then how his scowl went suddenly slack a few minutes later.

That's the moment he loves most of all—even more than the blood. The moment of knowing.

Knowing that something very bad is about to happen. And that it's too late to stop it.

CHAPTER 17

October 19

Taylor holds both tubes of fake blood up to the fluorescent lights overhead. One is a dark, viscous red. The other is brighter and looks runnier in the tube as she tilts it back and forth. "Guys, which one of these looks more real? Guys?"

When no one responds, she places both tubes of blood in her basket and peers into the next aisle. Maren and Jamie are standing in front of a full-length mirror, holding up costumes. Jamie's bottom lip is curled into a deep pout that makes her already high cheekbones look almost comical. Maren is pouting too, but only because she's making fun of Jamie—who hasn't noticed yet.

Maren zeroed in on a sexy skeleton costume right off the bat. Jamie is still debating between a sexy unicorn and a sexy devil.

Maren looks up and sees Taylor, waving her over to the mirror. She drops the pout and holds up the skeleton costume against her chest. "I guess I'll have to wear it with tights," she mutters, eyeing the short black skirt painted with glow-in-the-dark hip bones. Black-and-purple garters connect the hip bones on the skirt to the rib bones on the plunging drawstring corset. "Can I keep this at your house, Tay? I told my mom I was wearing the same costume as last year." Maren smiles crookedly.

Last year, Maren dressed up as a very modest black cat. Officially, anyway. As soon as she arrived at Taylor's house on Halloween, she'd exchanged her black sweatpants and sweatshirt for a skin-tight, sheer leotard and stripper boots. Taylor's dad was the designated cool parent in the group.

Taylor shrugs and plucks the tube of thick, dark blood out of her basket. She's pretty sure that real blood is on the thinner side. "Um, sure. My dad doesn't care. Jamie, how about you?"

Jamie deepens her pout and leans closer to the mirror. She holds both the devil and unicorn costumes against her chest. "Unicorns are still, like, a *thing,* right? It's not too middle school?"

Maren tugs on a lock of Jamie's auburn hair. "Unicorns are endlessly and forever cool. And with that mane, you're basically a boss-bitch unicorn already."

Jamie rolls her eyes and giggles but doesn't put the devil costume down. "But is it the *right* costume for the Thicket? I mean, it's just so . . . *wholesome.* I just feel like maybe I should go darker."

"Like . . . a zombie?" Taylor picks up the latex makeup kit and the remaining blood vial from her basket. She shakes them behind Jamie's reflection in the mirror. "Check this out. It's makeup, not a mask. So you could wear it to the Thicket and school." She tugs on the sleeve of Jamie's devil costume. "Come on. There's never just *one* zombie. I need a whole horde."

Jamie tosses her long hair as she turns to look. She frowns when she sees the photo on the cover of the latex kit Taylor is holding. Bloody strips of skin hang in ribbons from the model's cheeks, and her forehead is pocked with crusting red sores. It's incredible.

Jamie frowns. "It's just . . . Russ will see it. So I don't want to intentionally look, like, *bad*," she says with a shrug.

Taylor rolls her eyes and drops the makeup kit back in her basket. "Thanks."

Maren flips her feather-down blonde bangs to the side as she bats her thick black eyelashes. "You don't have to worry, James. *Bae* knows what you look like *under* your costume."

A woman in a faded pink tracksuit hurries by with a toddler clutching a tiger mask. The woman glances disapprovingly at Jamie, who has flung both costumes into her cart to tackle Maren. "Shhh," Jamie hisses, glancing at the hastily retreating backside of the woman in the tracksuit.

The Saturday morning after homecoming, Jamie had sent everyone a text saying she had "big news." However, she refused to share it until Monday morning. After gathering everyone in the bathroom after the first bell, she had solemnly announced that she and Russ had "made love" on Friday night after homecoming.

Maren had laughed so hard and so loud that a female teacher in the hallway heard and escorted them out into the hallway and back to class. Jamie had refused to talk to Maren for the rest of the day. This meant that Taylor got to hear all the juicy details of the La Quinta lovemaking first. Which was kind of fortuitous, since it meant she could ask all the questions Maren would have laughed at.

Maren had done it ages ago—freshman year—with a super-senior named Josh who exclusively wore cargo pants. Taylor assumes that Maren and Jamie know she is still a virgin since she's never actually admitted to anything beyond handsy make-out sessions. However, nobody has ever actually uttered the word "virgin," and Taylor prefers to keep it that way.

"Are we going to Maisie Barrett's party on Friday?" Maren asks, steering the cart toward the registers at the front of the store. Jamie reluctantly places the tiny unicorn costume back on the rack and throws the devil costume into her cart, then hurries to catch up.

Taylor shrugs, stopping to examine a display of false teeth. "I think we should skip Maisie's party and go to the Thicket that night instead. Maisie's boyfriend is trying to turn it into a pharm party. Apparently, Maisie's going along with it. She talks about her mom's stash of Xanax *all* the time."

Jamie grabs the edge of the cart and stops to examine a red sequined headband with plastic devil horns. "Russ knows Maisie pretty well. She's not going to turn it into a pharm party."

Maren pushes the cart forward again and smiles. "Well. If *Russ* says so." When Jamie gives her a dirty look, she laughs. "I'm freaking kidding. But I'm with Tay. Let's skip Maisie's and go to the Thicket on Friday. Saturday is going to be nuts. They're doing that dumb 'Double-Dog Scare' promo." She pulls her wallet from underneath the costumes at the bottom of the cart, quoting the radio ad: "Double the fun, half the price!" Ignoring Jamie's frown she adds, "Tay, could we stay the night at your house afterward? Will your dad care?"

Taylor shakes her head and grins. On paper, Scott Bennett is most aware of the risks teenagers take—and therefore most likely to worry. He's been a criminal defense lawyer at Hall, Blanton & Bennett for as long as Taylor can remember. Taylor can rattle off the stats on illegal drug use in Rupert, the average fine for a DUI, and the top three counties in Southeast Idaho for rape reports. But Scott's approach to parenting, like law, is innocent until proven guilty. In general, he's pretty content to treat Taylor and her friends like rational—albeit standard-issue—teenage girls. It's the unspoken agreement they've had since Taylor's mom, Wendy, moved to California with her new husband. And it's worked out fine.

While they stand in line for the one open register, Jamie scrolls through Snapchat. She suddenly shrieks, then laughs. "Oh my gosh. Quick, look."

Before the Snap disappears, Taylor and Maren lean in to see the grainy image on screen.

Taylor's stomach turns. It's a photo of a bloody eyeball. The photo Brandon took. A bubble caption at the bottom reads, "Old McDonald had a farm. HAD."

Taylor looks away. "I don't want to see that, you guys."

Maren pulls the phone closer. "It's not real, you know."

Taylor tries to make her voice lighter. "I know. It's just . . . *he* took the photo. That's all."

Maren shrugs. "You're gonna see it at the Thicket on Friday."

Jamie tucks the phone back into her purse. "Sorry, Tay."

Taylor feels her cheeks go red and pretends to study some glitter lip gloss near the counter. It's fake blood on a fake eyeball. Same as the vial in her basket. So why is her hand shaking? She wonders if Norah has seen all the memes. "Yeah, the effects are, uh, really good this year. I mean . . . I guess they must be, considering."

Maren plucks a tube of lip gloss from the stand near the register. "Maisie went the day the Thicket reopened. She said they've completely redone the room where it happened. Scrubbed it out, stuck some animatronic crap inside. There's a dedicated security guard stationed there now, too. Maisie said that if you bring a black light, you can still see some of the blood. But if they catch you, they'll confiscate the light."

Jamie shakes her head and puts the devil costume behind a bar at the register. "People are such freakin' morons. The Thicket is probably going to end up being totally lame. I mean, did you hear about the new 'security protocols'?"

Maren sighs and opens the lip gloss while the cashier frowns at her. "They only mention them in every single article. *No* masks, *no* backpacks, metal detectors, 3X security, we care about safety *so* much, *blah blah blah*."

Taylor giggles softly. "I heard Andy M. say he was trying to sell his beak mask on eBay for two hundred bucks, since he can't wear it to the Thicket now. He read a SocialBuzz article that said searches for 'Halloween beak masks' are up 2,000 percent."

Jamie rolls her eyes and hands her card to the cashier. "What if we hit the Thicket early on Friday night and then stopped by Maisie's party afterward. You know, if there's time? It gets dark by like five now. The lines are going to be shorter the earlier we go, anyway."

Maren places her sexy skeleton costume on the conveyor and smiles at the stone-faced cashier, who is pretending not to eavesdrop. "Let me guess—Russ is going to Maisie's party. Tell him to come to the Thicket with us instead."

Jamie shakes her head. "He said he doesn't want to go. His little brother Clark was science partners with Brandon. He's like, having a hard time with the whole thing. We're taking Clark trick-or-treating next weekend." Jamie holds up the sheer red fishnet tights for the devil costume and frowns. "Which means I can't wear this. So maybe I should join Taylor's zombie horde."

Taylor laughs and grabs Jamie's arm, pretending to take a bite. "I think it's adorable that he's taking his little brother trick-or-treating. And I don't care when we go to the Thicket. My dad might even let me drive us there if we go early enough on Friday, though."

Maren's face lights up. She signs her receipt with a flourish and grins. "Done. Let's do this, bitches."

CHAPTER 18

Norah refreshes the Facebook page for the Thicket's "Double-Dog Scare" event again. The names in the "going" and "maybe" sections blur before her eyes. They're the names of her classmates. She wouldn't call them friends. Especially not now.

They're all going to the Thicket this Saturday. For half price.

She pauses on some of the names, then keeps scrolling and refreshing. Three thousand people and counting have RSVPed.

The RSVP list includes Aaron, her pot dealer from Raft River, whose last text in her saved messages still reads, *Sry. Ur brother sounds like a D.*

It includes Maisie Barrett, who is also hosting a party on Friday night for the entire sophomore class.

And it includes Maren, Taylor, and Jamie.

Two weeks ago, Norah got a flurry of text messages, asking how she was doing. Some from numbers she didn't even recognize. Last week, she got three texts. This week zero. Not that she responded to any of them. Instead, she'd carefully rationed the last of her pot gummies, which is running dismally low. She might have to talk to Aaron again after all.

When Norah's mom forgot last week's counseling appointment, Norah didn't say anything. Instead, she fell asleep in the middle of the day, listening to The Smiths under the hazy, heavy comfort of a blackberry drop.

Norah wonders when she'll have to go back to school. Or go back to counseling. Could she refuse?

Norah shuts the laptop and glances at the empty key holder in the kitchen. Her dad is still at work. Her mom might be at the police station. Or her aunt's house. Or the moon. The house, as usual, is quiet except for the burbling of the aquarium in the living room. Norah hasn't looked at the fish lately.

Suddenly aware that she is actually hungry, Norah gets up and wanders downstairs into the kitchen. When she opens the cupboards, she's surprised to see a few new groceries on the splintering shelves. It's been more than two weeks since anyone has cooked dinner, let alone eaten a meal together. Every interaction revolves around the logistics of press conferences, police updates, and news articles. Which is slightly better than funeral plans, flowers, and burial plots.

The people who texted last week all said the same thing. That they "couldn't imagine" what Norah was going through. Norah remembers saying the phrase herself more than once. *Before.* When the phrase sounded like, "I'm so sorry this happened to you." Now all she hears is, "I'm so glad this happened to you, not me."

Honestly, what's to imagine? It's a black hole.

She hesitates then picks up a jar of spaghetti sauce. The fridge is stacked with casseroles and leftovers that have trickled into the fridge after the funeral. Some of them are definitely still edible. But the mishmash of half-eaten, unfamiliar pans and trays in her fridge fills Norah's stomach with a queasy feeling.

She decides she'll make pasta. It's one of the few meals she feels confident in making without asking for instructions.

A few minutes later, there's a pot of water boiling on the stovetop and a saucepan bubbling beside it, sending waves of steam across the peeling black plastic of the microwave above it.

Norah moves through the kitchen on autopilot, salting the water, pulling plates from the cupboard for her mom and dad.

When the noodles are cooked, she drains them in the sink, carefully ladles them onto a plate, and pours the sauce and a sprinkle of parmesan on top.

She closes her eyes and tries to live in the smell of the warm food. To be present, like the counselor talked about. And for a moment, it works. When she opens her eyes, she considers calling her mom's cell phone to ask where she is and if she'd like some dinner. Or at least a saved plate.

But just like the curls of steam wafting from the hot plate, the notion disappears.

Sometimes, Norah feels like her family members are living in different dimensions. Or maybe different circles of hell. She doesn't feel abandoned. Or resentful. She just accepts that they can't reach each other right now.

Norah listens for the garage door for a few seconds as if her mom might arrive on cue. The ice maker hums in the quiet, in tune with the aquarium pump. Outside, the wind has picked up, and she can hear dead leaves scatter across the deck in a soft, brittle rasping sound.

Norah pulls a fork from the dishwasher and sits at the table by herself. The willow branches are scraping back and forth across the fence, a sound like sandpaper.

She peers out the sliding glass door. But in the glare of the Tiffany lamp over the kitchen table, all she sees is her own reflection. She studies her bare face and limp hair then turns away.

After a couple bites of pasta, Norah stands up, covers her plate with plastic wrap, and shoves aside two casserole dishes in the fridge to make room for it.

Norah's mom has been calling about the autopsy report for the past two weeks. First asking. Then demanding. Then threatening to speak to the press. She'd threatened to bring it up in her interview with Channel Two. And in the press conference with the police.

The Rupert PD were already taking heat for their failure to identify the man in the security footage at the Thicket. They had him on camera, for god's sake. So after two weeks of threats, they finally relented and agreed to send the portions of the autopsy that weren't critical to the investigation.

When Norah saw the thick envelope clutched in her mom's hands yesterday, she knew what it was. And when Norah was alone in the house, she spent an hour searching until she found the envelope. Because she needed to know.

Massive blood loss due to laceration of the C1 vertebrae aggravated by asphyxia.

Sharp force trauma to the base of the skull.

That was the official cause of death. There were no defensive wounds. Either the guy who did it had come up behind him. Or Brandon had tried to run away. Either way, he hadn't stood a chance.

Because he was alone. The autopsy doesn't say that, of course. It doesn't need to.

Norah had read the entire autopsy. Twice. And snippets of the clinical phrases had permanently committed themselves to a loop in her mind. She'd finally used up the last of her stash of pot to make them stop so she could fall asleep. She won't be able to avoid texting Aaron soon.

The lingering smell of the spaghetti sauce suddenly makes Norah queasy, and she retreats to the basement. As she walks down the stairs, she's unable to stop herself from glancing at the carefully constructed gallery of photos in the stairway. The wall is packed with Norah and Brandon's chronological school pictures. His hair was too long in this year's photo, curling over his ears in blunt blonde tufts. He hated having it cut.

Norah tries to find the sadness. The grief. Even the anger she felt when she was looking at the Facebook event earlier. But it's like trying to pull a too-big anchor aboard into a too-small boat. It will capsize her, where the ocean will swallow her whole. So all she feels are the few bites of spaghetti she took roiling in her stomach. And a whisper that reminds her at every turn: *Your fault.*

The basement smells musty and undisturbed. The carpet is original to the house, and so is the peeling floral wallpaper her parents always talked about ripping out. They moved here the year Brandon was six and Norah was ten. In the corner, behind one side of the couch, is an ancient treadmill her mom found at a garage sale in Burley two summers ago. To Norah's knowledge, none of them have ever actually used it.

She plugs the machine in and is surprised to see the display light up. As the conveyor begins to move, Norah hesitantly steps on it with her bare feet. It takes all of two minutes before she is breathing heavily, her lungs burning.

She turns the speed up and adjusts the incline until the machine maxes out with a thin groan. She wouldn't say it feels good. But it's better than doing nothing. Better than feeling herself take easy breaths.

Asphyxiate.

Norah turns up the speed on the treadmill. In her search for the autopsy report yesterday, she found another thick manila folder on her mom's desk. It contained every article that had been published about the Thicket over the past three weeks. There were forty-three in total. The first one had been published the day after the murders. A sticky note on the first folder had a phone number and the name "Officer Albright" written in her mother's neat handwriting.

The articles had titles like, "10 of the Most Haunted Places in America." and "25 Real Haunted Houses in the Northwest." The Thicket was featured as number one in that particular article, with a photo of the caution tape and an ambulance inside the main plaza. Norah recognized most of the titles. She's made anonymous comments on most of them.

Before Norah hits the red STOP button on the treadmill, she promises herself she won't check anyone's Facebook page. Or refresh the RSVPs to the Thicket's "Double Dog Scare" event. For someone who deleted her own Facebook account, she spends a lot of time there. If she stays on the treadmill long enough, she might even be able to fall asleep without texting Aaron for more weed. Her feet are blistering under the rubber.

Twenty minutes later, she can hear the faint rumble of the garage door opening. Her dad is home. She hears him open the door and set his keys on the counter. Then the quiet whoosh of the refrigerator door, the clank of glass, and the chirp of the microwave. She slows the treadmill down to a normal pace.

A few minutes later, she hears footsteps in the kitchen again. They hesitate at the landing. "Norah, honey?" she hears over the whir of the conveyor belt. "Did you make the spaghetti?"

When she doesn't answer, the footsteps slowly retreat. She thinks she hears him add, "Thank you."

Relief, then guilt, then apathy wash over her in waves that disappear as quickly as they arise.

When she hears the bedroom door shut upstairs, she finally presses the STOP button on the treadmill. The machine whirs to a stop, and the room is quiet again.

Sweaty and shaking hard, Norah steps off the treadmill and moves toward the closed bedroom door down the hallway before she can think too much about it.

His bed still isn't made. The red-and-blue flannel comforter is rumpled, pushed all the way down to the bottom of the bed, and the sheets are dirty.

She doesn't lay down on the bed, though.

Instead, she pulls the neatly folded quilt from the top closet shelf. The one their nana made for Brandon when he was born. It has bright yellow tractors, excavators, graders, and bulldozers crisscrossing the fabric.

Norah turns off the bedroom light, unfolds the quilt, and settles into the cushions of the overstuffed brown recliner in the corner of the room.

She can't smell his smell anymore in the room. There is just the musty basement aroma. For a moment, she considers walking to his bed to lay her head on his pillow to inhale and reassure herself that she'll still be able to find him here. But the thought that he might not be there anymore either keeps her where she is.

Sometimes it's better not to know.

She should shower. Or at least change her clothes. Her T-shirt is damp, and her feet hurt. But her eyes are closing. And the clammy goosebumps on her arms barely even register.

CHAPTER 19

October 19th

He meets Janet's smile as she hobbles along the sidewalk toward the breezeway entrance. He opens the door a little wider to accommodate the width of her walker.

"Now, you didn't have to stand there in the cold like that, with me moving like molasses," Janet titters, the corners of her eyes creasing so deeply that her dark brown eyes are nearly hidden.

He shakes his head in a gesture that is both gracious and humble as she inches the walker past him.

She pauses her amble to pat his arm. "I'm always telling my oldest granddaughter about you, you know. Sharice. Such a pretty thing. Well-endowed too." She winks and nudges his arm conspiratorially. "Just graduated from college. Needs a nice young man in her life."

Her smile obscures her eyes again, and he chuckles obligingly. "Oh, I don't know about the young part, Mrs. Tanner. And you know me, I'm a lone wolf."

She swats at him and calls to the petite redhead walking up the path to the apartment building. The redhead is carrying a sack of groceries in the crook of one arm and a squirming baby on her hip. "Lisa, tell our handsome neighbor that he's selfishly denying my granddaughter of a baby like that." Janet takes one hand off her walker to gesture at the baby, who is reaching for her mother's hair. "Or least a date."

The redhead—Lisa—sets the bag of groceries in a heap at their feet and laughs, casting a sidelong glance in his direction. She extricates a fistful of hair from the baby's chubby hand. "Janet, if your granddaughter is half as sweet as you are, he'd be crazy to turn you down." The baby squirms harder, porpoising in her arms, reaching for that red hair again.

On a whim, he hunches down, placing himself at eye level with the little girl's tiny face. She studies him with wide, blue eyes for a moment, assessing him.

When her face breaks out in a gummy grin, he reaches out to gently stroke her cheek, grazing the soft skin near her temple. He can see the blue blood rush in and out of the veins beneath her tissue-thin skin.

He wonders how hard he would have to press to break the surface.

Beside him, Janet coos at the two of them softly, clucking over what a wonderful father he would be. As Lisa bends down to retrieve the sack of groceries, the baby arches back against her mother's shoulder and succeeds in seizing another fistful of hair, ignoring him again.

He straightens and smiles. Just as well. Too close to home.

Lisa picks up her groceries and starts up the stairwell, patiently working to extricate the lock of hair from her baby's grip. "I swore I'd never cut my hair after having kids. So typical. But I'm calling uncle." She laughs at her own joke and waves goodbye. "Have a good day, you two. And let Janet set you up!"

He smiles. Lisa is about the same age as the blond news anchor. Caroline. And she's just as clueless. *Oh, Caroline. You think you're so savvy. But you'd let the* perpetrator *kiss your baby, too.*

Taking the opportunity to exit the building without seeming rude, he waves back at Lisa and pats Janet gently on the shoulder as he walks out the breezeway.

The sky is cloudless, and the air is crisp and electric. He feels good as he walks the five blocks to the second-hand home improvement store and buys what he needs. He's pleased he thought to come here. There are no security cameras. And even if there were, there is nothing remotely unusual about a customer buying rope, Gorilla tape, and a utility knife.

The high-school-aged girl at the counter, wearing a green vest, doesn't even look up as he studies the hand-labeled prices.

He smiles as he gives her the crisp bills he withdrew from the ATM yesterday, then strides back out the door.

He'll be home in time to watch the six o'clock news. Now that the Thicket has reopened without incident, the top breaking stories aren't about him anymore.

He gently touches the utility knife inside the brown paper sack.

That'll change soon enough.

CHAPTER 20

October 21

RealityTV has just announced that it will be releasing a made-for-TV docudrama about the "Thicket Tragedy."

This morning, the producers called to ask if Norah's family would be willing to be interviewed.

Norah's mom said yes.

Norah squeezes her eyes shut and tries to turn off the static in her mind.

They didn't ask to interview Norah. Because nobody aside from the police actually knows she was there that night. Let alone that she's the reason Brandon is dead. That she left him to wander through the Thicket alone. To be attacked from behind. Because she was annoyed with him.

Norah squeezes her eyes shut again, and tries to visualize the stretch of trail where she left him. The staff exit she took back to the plaza through the woods. But there is only blank static. Norah isn't sure whether that's because she really can't remember or because her brain is hiding some dark truth from her.

The feature image for the *RealityTV* documentary shows a partially open door to Cabin Twelve. There's crime scene tape surrounding the entire structure. It's the same image the Internet has passed around. If you zoom in and increase the resolution, you can see that the threshold of the doorway is stained red.

Norah closes the tab and refreshes the "Double Dog Scare" Facebook event, which is happening on Saturday. There are a couple hundred more RSVPs.

She imagines showing up at the Thicket's event the way she sometimes imagines tipping her body over the edge of the railing at Shoshone Falls.

She would never do it, of course.

But would she?

A lifetime ago, while the Thicket was still closed and still surrounded by caution tape and red-and-blue lights, Norah had made the drive out to Declo.

She had parked near the far end of the corn maze, on a narrow gravel road that ran beside a weed-choked canal. Just ahead, she could see a dilapidated farmhouse, a trailer, and a barbed-wire fence where a few chickens ducked in and out, picking at weeds.

From this border of the Thicket, it was all cornfields, waving gently in the early October sunlight. The sky was so cloudless and blue it hurt to look at. When she craned her neck, she could just see the top of one of the bigger cabins. Nothing else.

Norah wasn't sure why she went back. Wasn't sure what she expected to feel. Or to see. But after fifteen minutes, a police car had pulled up behind her on the canal road. The officer rested his hand lightly on his hip, above his holster, tapping on the trunk of her Buick as he motioned for her to roll down the window.

For a horrifying moment, Norah was worried he would know who she was. That his expression would soften in pity and remorse. But of course, he didn't recognize her. Why would he? She nodded when he chastised her for parking on the private access road near the crime scene. Hadn't she seen Wind River's "no access" sign on the main road?

Like every year, the Thicket will close the day after Halloween. When the cleanup crew is finished, there will be nothing but dead cornfields, empty cabin shells, and acres of hiking trails marred with the occasional checkered wrapper.

The room where Brandon died will be locked and fenced off like all the other cabins, until next year.

She knows from several different articles that the room where it happened has been basically gutted. Scoured. Redecorated.

She also knows from the articles that have popped up all over Facebook that several groups of kids walked through Cabin Twelve *before* Brandon died—but *after* the other staffer had been killed. The person who did this was waiting for someone to enter the cabin alone. He was waiting for someone vulnerable.

Someone who wouldn't have been alone if Norah had stayed with him.

When the police asked Norah why she left Brandon, she had a hard time remembering the conversation that had sent her stomping through the exit trail to the plaza. And that was when she felt the numbness spread through her body like insulation.

Norah closes the tab on the "Double Dog Scare" event and opens Messenger. She's not Facebook friends with Aaron. Or anyone else, really, on this fake account. But "Ashlyn Palmer" has a profile photo of a dimpled brunette who appears to attend Burley High School. She's totally Aaron's type.

Taking a deep breath, Norah types out a message before she can think about it too much. "Hey! Sorry for the random message. One of my friends told me maybe you could, you know, hook me up?"

Almost instantly, she is notified that Aaron has seen the message. And he is typing a response.

"Heyyyyy. No prob. Watchu want."

Norah exhales slowly with relief. "$50. Anything edible." He's already typing before she sends the response.

"U in Burley? Can u pick up?"

Norah's heart rate speeds up. Aaron lives in the tiny town of Albion. Which means she'll have to skirt past Declo on her way there and back. She clicks the "send money" icon in messenger and waits for the confirmation ping. Then she replies, "$$ sent. My weekend is kinda crazy. Can you leave it somewhere for me?"

The little dots appear and reappear, indicating that Aaron is typing and erasing. Norah holds her breath, regretting the too-cute photo of the girl with the dimples. He'd be far less likely to want to meet up with a skinny dude with braces.

Finally, his response appears. "K. Ya. Water tower, Friday? U know it?"

Norah feels her chest tighten just a little. Of course she knows it. That's where she last saw him. When she decided to skip homeroom in favor of meeting up with him and Kenny. "Yep. Just leave it behind the painted rock ok? LMK when."

Her eyes blur as the dots on screen dance in front of her eyes for several seconds. Then: "Coo. Will leave it tmrw after school. LMK if u want more or wanna meet up sometime? I like ur pic."

Norah's stomach twists. She "likes" the message then shuts the laptop.

There is a lonely sliver of blackberry gummy left in the plastic bag in Norah's nightstand. Before, she used to keep her stash in the top of her closet, inside the toe of a pair of snow boots. She remembers the panic she felt when she thought about her parents—or Brandon—finding it.

She'd give anything to worry about that again.

Through her half-open bedroom door, Norah can see the light of the TV flickering beneath her parents' bedroom door.

Without bothering to get up and shut her own door, she pops the gummy in her mouth. Then she puts her headphones in and skips through songs until she hears the opening chords of "Suffer the Little Children."

The dark lyrics are strangely soothing. Three bodies have been found on the moors. Lesly Ann is dead. John is dead. Edward is dead—but not forgotten. Because wherever his soul has gone, his mother's soul is there too.

CHAPTER 21

October 23

"Do you want me to curl your hair while you finish your makeup, Mare?" Jamie asks.

Maren is sitting on top of the vanity in her strapless bra and underwear, her feet in the sink and her face inches from the mirror. She finishes applying a second coat of purple lipstick, purses her lips, and turns around to look at Jamie. "James, I swear to god I'm almost done. We'll be out of here by five o'clock at the latest. Will you go watch TV or something? You're making me nervous."

The plan had been to get ready together. However, Jamie had shown up with her fake eyelashes and devil costume already on, casually suggesting that if they left sooner than planned, they'd have to spend even less time waiting in line at the Thicket.

Jamie ignores Maren's pointed question and adjusts her cleavage in the mirror. The sexy devil costume consists of a revealing red bustier with two red triangles of fabric fanning down from the hips. Taylor assumes it's supposed to be a skirt. There's also a matching headband with sequined red horns and slinky fishnet stockings. "I'm totally fine with whatever," Jamie says nonchalantly. She runs a hand through her auburn hair, which falls in sheets down her nearly bare back. "But Annie went just last weekend, and she had to wait, like, an hour just to get her ticket."

Taylor rolls her eyes. "Annie also told us she got her period when she was five. We'll be fine. Some kid in my math class said he went last night and hardly had to wait in line at all." She dabs a layer of green greasepaint over the black-and-white layer she drew around her eyes. She rubs the paint until it blends into a mottled, sickly gray that highlights the latex scars she applied earlier. She reaches for the vial of thin, red blood and drizzles a little down her cheeks, letting the liquid drip onto her T-shirt.

Maren hops off the vanity and grabs her costume from the dresser. She eases her arms into the cheap fabric of the black and purple corset then works the laces through the metal loops and pulls them as tight as she can. "Maisie's party doesn't even start until seven. Why are we rushing?"

Jamie continues to study her reflection in the mirror, chest out, lips pursed, eyes narrowed in a calculated smolder. And then she abruptly deflates, flopping down to sit on the toilet seat with her chin in her hands. "I'm sorry, you guys. Some bitch in math has been flirting with Russ. She's going to be at Maisie's party tonight. And get this: She's dressing up as an *angel*. A freakin' *angel*. I know it's probably nothing. I mean, after homecoming and everything . . . but it's still making me crazy, you know? Like, get your *own* man."

"Aw, I'm sorry, James." Taylor puts the vial of blood down. "But you seriously don't have anything to worry about. I've seen the way Russ looks at you, and he has 100 percent sold his soul to the devil." She wiggles her paint-crusted eyebrows up and down, nudging Jamie with her foot.

Jamie groans at the joke but sits up a little straighter on the toilet. "You really think that? I mean, we've only been *officially* dating for a few weeks, but—"

Maren, who has successfully finished lacing her corset, strides over and plucks Jamie's phone out of her hands. "Look in the mirror again, James. Like you were a few minutes ago."

Jamie gives her a suspicious look. "Why?"

Maren sighs. "Just do it. Trust me."

When Jamie reluctantly stands, Maren deftly adjusts a few strands of Jamie's hair and tugs down on the hem of the bright red corset. "Boobs out. Okay, now *smolder*."

Maren angles the phone up and snaps a flurry of photos then examines the results. She taps on the screen and hands the phone back to Jamie. "There. Send him that one, right now. He'll lose his shit. And then can you please help me curl my hair? I hate it right now." She grimaces at her stick-straight pixie cut in the mirror.

Taylor smiles as she slips into a pair of ratty jeans and her dad's old BSU sweatshirt. He has graciously allowed her to shred with a pair of scissors and smear it with some of the blood and greasepaint.

The zombie costume looks good, she decides, studying her reflection in the mirror. Out of the corner of her eye, she studies Maren, who is struggling to bend over in the tight corset as she reaches for the curling iron.

Last year, Taylor dressed up as Amelia Earhart. Jamie and Maren were sexy witches. As far as Taylor can remember, the last time Maren or Jamie wore a costume without the word "sexy" in front of it was fifth grade, the end of elementary school.

That was also the year Wendy Bennett filed for divorce and moved to Boise, three hours away. The move was necessary to launch her interior design business. "There are exactly 2,204 houses in Rupert," Wendy had said. "And that's counting the trailers."

Wendy had come back to Rupert twice that year. Once when she had an appointment with a client in Idaho Falls. And once when she returned to break the news that she was moving to California with her boyfriend Nick.

Idaho is so small, she had said. *I'm suffocating here.* When Wendy stopped by the house for the last time, she'd been wearing pale pink, pointed-toe pumps, skinny jeans with a chic line of rips down one knee, and a tailored black blazer. "You sure you don't want to come with me, hon?" she'd asked Taylor, leaning in for a quick side hug on the porch as she peered into the house.

Wendy had reached out to touch the silver bar necklace Taylor was wearing. "It would be fun," she said, stroking Taylor's hair. "Nick *loves* you. And I've lost so much weight, people will think we're sisters."

When Wendy left, she planted a soft, glossy kiss on Taylor's cheek and muttered a goodbye to Taylor's dad through the screen door. As if he hadn't been standing a few feet away the whole time.

After she was gone, Taylor had locked herself in the bathroom and looked at her reflection in the mirror. Her thick, straight nose and wavy brown hair came from her dad. Her "elf-bite" ears and hazel eyes had undeniably come from Wendy. That would always be true. Not that it seemed to matter much.

Taylor had stared at her reflection until it blurred in front of her eyes. And then she'd carefully removed the silver bar necklace Wendy had sent her for her birthday and buried it at the bottom of the bathroom trash can.

"All right, bitches. What are we doing for dinner?" Maren asks from the vanity, where she's resumed her perch. Jamie is standing behind her with the curling iron, wrapping the last of Maren's blond hair into short, spiral curls. "I assume you're ready to go, Tay?

Taylor scrutinizes herself in the mirror with a smirk. "You mean you can't tell whether I'm ready?" She actually spent quite a bit of time on the messy braid tied with a dirty red ribbon and streaked with green from the greasepaint. But it's definitely not sexy.

When Jamie and Maren don't respond, Taylor leans against the closet door and peers at her reflection in the mirror, wondering if she should do something else with the braid. "My dad left us some money. We can eat in the plaza or grab something on the drive. Is there anything good in Declo now?"

"Plaza!" Jamie yelps, yanking Maren's head back with the curling iron that is still attached to a lock of her hair.

"Ow! Calm down, James. *Jesus.* Are the food trucks in the plaza even open this year? Or did they like, shut down the food stands too? You know, in case somebody gets stabbed with a caramel apple stick."

Jamie grimaces and hurries to unroll the last curl wrapped around the barrel of the curling iron. Taylor sits cross-legged on the closet floor, careful not to let the fake blood on her jeans touch the carpet. "I'd risk a stabbing.

Caramel apples sound so good. And the food trucks are still up and running—I checked the website after school. There's just a metal detector and stuff at the entrance. No big bags allowed." She grins and picks at a blob of fake blood that hasn't quite dried yet. "Mare, your corset is probably going to set off the metal detectors."

Maren smiles and casts a sideways glance at Taylor. "God I'm sexy. And your dad is awesome, Taylor. Tell him thanks for the money."

Taylor nods, feeling in her pocket for the keys and the wadded-up bills to make sure she didn't leave them in her other pair of pants before she changed.

Maren leans back on the counter, wrinkles her nose, and spritzes her curls with hairspray one more time. Jamie nods approvingly. They'll be on the road in a few minutes.

Taylor feels an unexpected fizz of excitement in her stomach, wondering what it will feel like to stand in the same room where it happened. There's no end to the reports about what Cabin Twelve looks like now, and what it feels like to be standing inside. Some kids say that the air feels heavier. Some say that you can still smell the blood—and worse. Other kids bring black lights that, before they're confiscated by security, show faintly glowing traces of residue on the scabby log walls.

Taylor's not sure what to expect. She's willing to bet money that the scariest new development at the Thicket is the new security guards. Cranky men who hate their day jobs—and kids too—shuffling everyone through as quickly as possible.

Maisie Barrett says that the bathtub scene has been replaced with a jail cell and robotic inmates rattling their chains. By all reports, it's the anti-climax of the Thicket. No actors. Just security guards in the cabin itself.

Still, that fizz in Taylor's stomach intensifies. She's never set foot in an actual crime scene before. Especially a crime scene like this. She knows plenty of kids who have returned to the reopened Thicket this year. And after the uneventful reopening, even the petitions to close the attraction down are losing steam.

Taylor's not actually worried that something bad might happen to her. In fact, some part of her recognizes that it's a little disappointing knowing that something certainly won't. But that feeling of staring into the dark and wondering if there's danger lurking there, even just a little danger, will never get old. It's the whole point of Halloween.

Jamie is glancing anxiously between Maren, who is still perched on the vanity, and the hallway to the garage. Taylor can't help but smile again.

"Come on, let's get the hell out of here," Maren says as she hops off the vanity. Jamie looks visibly relieved.

Without bothering to switch off the curling iron, Jamie trots down the hall toward the door, long red curls and devil tail swinging. "Shotgun!" she yells.

Maren tucks one last strand of wispy blond hair behind her ear and rolls her eyes as she turns off the curling iron. She smiles at Taylor. "Come on, Ms. *Walking Dead*. Let's go."

CHAPTER 22

He holds the knife against his palm, pressing down just a little.

Then a little more, until the skin turns white.

All blades are unique. It's important to know how much pressure is needed before they break the skin.

The answer, in most cases, is a bit harder than you'd think. You have to want to.

He'd hoped to find a high-end box cutter. Maybe an electrician's knife. It was impossible to anticipate exactly what you might come across in the tools section of the second-hand home improvement store. That was part of the fun. But there it was, slightly separated from the crush of saw blades, hammers, and box cutters jumbled across the plywood shelving, as if it were waiting for him to walk by.

The label, with the hand-scrawled yellow price tag, read "utility knife, $4." But anyone—perhaps with the exception of the high-school-age clerk—could see that this was, in fact, a mid-sized hunting knife. The three raised notches on the back were ideal for tearing through the thick, leathery hide of a deer or elk. The gut hook at the top was made for carefully opening the abdominal cavity to remove the delicate entrails without nicking the stomach or liver. And the thick blade that ended in a slight curve was meant for skinning and boning.

He's never actually killed anything with a hunting knife. Sporting goods stores and gun shops were dangerous. High traffic. Security cameras. Inventory that's tracked through sophisticated electronic programs. Not to mention, the staff were usually paid on commission. They always stood like prairie dogs in the entryways, scanning for the next potential customer, eager to strike up a conversation about the gun, the knife, or the rope. He'll take the debris pile at the second-hand corner store any day.

He trails his finger along the gut hook, pressing in on the sharp point. While he's never actually used a hunting knife, the first time he held one was a formative experience.

He'd seen the truck in the neighbors' driveway the night before. Saw the hunting tarps, blinds, and coolers being loaded up for an early morning departure.

He'd decided to tag along. That night, he set an alarm for 4:00 am to watch for signs of activity next door.

His parents didn't wake up when he eased the front door shut. And he was confident they wouldn't worry if they discovered him missing later. They never did.

When he'd walked up the driveway with a hopeful smile and his backpack, the glance between father and son was unmistakable. He hardly knew the neighbor boy, who was two years older in school. But social convention won out, as it usually did. Especially when he offered to wake up his parents to verify that he did, indeed have permission to tag along. Within the hour he was seated in the small cab of the truck, along for the ride.

They hadn't let him touch the guns, of course. He didn't have a license. But they'd handed him the knife. "You can skin it for us," the father had laughed in a booming voice, clearly hoping to dampen his enthusiasm.

It hadn't.

They'd made the kill at dusk. The son's first. A small buck with just one antler. A "unicorn," the father had called it, slapping the son on the back as the animal crashed through the brush, a river of red streaming down its arched neck as it disappeared.

They'd followed the chaos and the trail of bright blood for maybe a quarter of a mile, to a stand of trees. The deer lay crouched beside a poplar, knees buckled, neck bent forward.

He'd moved toward the animal with the knife. But before he could get far, the father had grabbed the collar of his shirt. "Not so fast. He might look half dead, but he's still got plenty of fight left in him."

The animal lay kneeling in the dirt, its glassy eyes looking back at them. Still alive. Afraid. But unable to run away.

The newly cleaned metal of the second-hand hunting knife flashes silver in the dim blue light of his computer screen. Vinegar, the nylon straps of his backpack, and a soft cloth have turned the steel blade smooth and spotless again. It's probably sharper now than it was new.

He appreciates small tools. Ordinary tools. Personal tools. Tools that belong on a workbench or a kitchen counter or a sportsman's backpack. Tools that sit on a shelf looking impotent in a second-hand shop, waiting for the right hand to pick them up.

But even ordinary tools will set off a metal detector.

He opens the dusty green backpack at his feet and places the knife inside.

Metal detectors don't fail.

But the people operating them do.

CHAPTER 23

When the syrupy smell of cotton candy hits her in the crowded parking lot, Norah almost gets back in her car.

This is a bad idea. There's no question about that. But with the buzz she has going from the strawberry drop she took half an hour ago, she rationalizes that driving is a worse idea.

Aaron wasn't waiting for her at the water tower, thank god. But Norah wore her dad's sweats—the ones that are so big they look like Hammer pants—and a hoodie pulled tight over her chin, just in case. Not that Aaron would have easily recognized her. She hasn't worn eyeliner or eyeshadow in weeks, which means that she looks like a squinty naked mole-rat.

Through the smoky half-darkness, beyond the crush of cars in the grassy lot, Norah can just see the line to the ticket trailer. It snakes past the bales of hay that form a wall around the perimeter of the Thicket, spilling into the first row of the teeming parking lot.

All of the kids in line are waiting for an hour on a Friday night to pay twenty bucks a piece to see the room where her brother died.

The black hole in the pit of Norah's stomach seems to expand as she walks through the roped-off lanes. As the brittle wind picks up, she imagines watching people turn, one by one, to look in her direction. To find out why the air has suddenly turned heavy.

Nobody does, of course. Instead, they crane their necks eagerly toward the ticket trailer at the other end of the parking lot and shriek as the wind whips up debris in tiny dust devils at their feet. They laugh and poke each other. They squeal as dark figures in masks and hoods weave through the line. They stamp their feet up and down to get warm in their skimpy costumes as they huddle together near the blazing orange fire barrels every few yards. They are silent and oblivious, bent over their phones while they wait.

Norah stops walking and looks back at the dark parking lot, vaguely wondering if she'll remember where her car is parked. Third row? Maybe halfway across the lot. There aren't any marked sections, just an endless loop of rope held up by white plastic poles—many of which are now lying horizontally in the grass.

She shrugs. The information has tipped into the black hole.

In the distance behind her, a steady line of blinding headlights inch forward toward the parking lot flagger wearing a reflective vest. Norah touches the cold rectangle of her phone lying in the kangaroo pouch of her hoodie. There are now 3,500 RSVPs to "Double Dog Scare" tomorrow night. But that's tomorrow.

Norah realizes that it has started snowing. Just a little. Unseasonably early, tiny flakes that could easily be mistaken for rain if not for the shifting beams of light cutting through the night air. The flakes fill her with an unexpected sense of nostalgia as they dance through the headlights.

"You're so high," Norah whispers to herself as she glances back in the direction of the car again. She thinks about texting her mom, telling her they should watch *Schitt's Creek* together tonight. The new season has been out for a while. She imagines microwaving a bag of popcorn and dragging the enormous afghan from the couch into her parents' bedroom like they used to do. It might be nice.

And then Norah hears the screams.

Shrill and distant. First one. Then a long, lingering chorus.

She closes her eyes while the buzz from the strawberry drop pulls the screams directly into the black hole.

They're not real screams. They can't hurt her.

After a few moments, Norah opens her eyes. She watches as the end of the ticket line creeps further around the edge of the hay bale wall.

She doesn't actually want to be at home watching TV.

The only place she really wants to be is here—but five weeks ago. To ruffle his too-long hair and roll her eyes instead of leaving him alone. To be counted among the kids who walked right through Cabin Twelve—and then later realized that the blood in the bathtub was real.

Norah knows that it's not possible to go back in time. She knows that finishing the trail tonight won't change anything. She knows it won't bring him back. But she also knows that she owes him this much.

And if it's awful, fine. Nobody is punishing her for what she did. So she'll punish herself.

Norah steadies herself then walks past the last row of parked cars. She makes her way down a dirt path running parallel to the ticket line, toward the end of the queue.

The line wraps around the hay wall enclosing the main plaza. The kids in line are separated into clusters every few feet, where the glowing fire barrels cast slim circles of warmth. She can just see the end of the line from here.

The bruise-purple sky is still spitting tiny flecks of white, just visible in the licking flames that curl over the edge of the fire barrels.

As she continues toward the end of the ticket line, Norah makes eye contact with a girl who can't be much older than ten—younger than Brandon.

The girl smiles and adjusts the hem of her sequined tube top, leaning away from the fire barrel as she fluffs the bangs on her purple wig. Then she grabs her friend's arm, whispering something in her ear that makes them both giggle. The friend is dressed as a vampire, with rivulets of blood painted on the corners of her mouth.

Norah pulls the strings of her hoodie tighter. When the girls don't sneak a second glance, Norah breathes a sigh of relief. They weren't talking about her ginormous sweatpants or Unabomber hoodie. Or the fact that she's probably not walking in the straightest line.

As if on cue, a man directly behind the girls glances up at Norah.

He's older, with gray hair curling around his ears and a thick, untrimmed beard. He's wearing army fatigues and a puffy down coat. Norah can't tell if he's Army or if this is a costume. Based on his proximity to the girl in the purple wig, he's her dad.

The man smiles weakly at Norah before turning back to his daughter.

Norah looks at the ground and hurries away, digging her fingernails into her palms. *Don't look at anyone else,* she instructs herself. *Just walk to the end of the line.*

CHAPTER 24

The drive to Declo takes longer than Taylor anticipated. She knows that part of the problem is how slowly she's driving. When her dad offered to let her drive tonight, the clocks were still an hour ahead. By the time they hit the road tonight, the sky was nearly dark.

The lack of streetlights and endless black hills make Taylor feel like even her brights can't cut through the darkness. Rupert isn't a metropolis by any means. Right now, anyone who isn't at Maisie's party or headed to the Thicket on Friday night is cruising the short drag between the I-84 and the presbyterian church, or packed into the Taco Bell.

But out here, where the scraggly foothills are dotted with town names that most people have never heard of—Malta, Albion, Sublet, Almo, Elba—even the side roads and sidewalks disappear. The sparse, dilapidated manufactured homes and crumbling barns tucked just off the road—does anyone live in them anymore?

Deep purple clouds sit heavily along the dark horizon where the last slip of sunlight has turned the sky deep pink.

"I'm turning the music down just a little," Taylor murmurs, twisting the radio dial as a few flecks of white appear on the windshield. Jamie and Maren don't notice. They're looking at Maren's Instagram account now and shrieking when the phone loses service. Another set of headlights blazes into view, making Taylor squint.

Scanning the shoulder of the road for a place that's safe to pull over a little, Taylor slows down even more and lets the other vehicle pass before the driver starts flashing their lights. From the passenger seat, Jamie looks up from her phone and sighs. "Are you sure you don't want me to drive, Tay?"

Taylor shakes her head as a reflective green and white sign comes into view. *Declo: 5 miles.* Thank god. She can feel her fingers cramping up from her vise grip on the steering wheel. "We're almost there."

As they crest the next dip in the road, Taylor can see a long line of red tail-lights just ahead. The turnoff is marked by an unassuming, hand-painted wooden sign staked at the edge of a mowed field. *Thicket: ¼ mile.*

Maren and Jamie put their phones down as the car creeps forward in the long line at the Thicket's parking entrance. Maren pulls a tube of lipstick from her purse and flips open the dash mirror as Taylor squints into the darkness, looking for an empty parking space. She breathes a sigh of relief as she follows the line of tail-lights in a slow serpentine pattern through the enormous dirt parking lot. At least nobody expects her to drive faster here.

Beyond the hay bales surrounding the parking lot, the now-dark sky is lit up with strobing lights. The music from the DJ booth is so loud she can hear the lyrics inside the car.

They finally find an empty spot six rows back in the crooked rows of cars parked on the matted dirt and grass. Maren rolls down her window a few inches, putting her hand up to feel the outside air. "Jesus, that's cold. I'm bringing my coat." The music from the DJ booth gets louder. Immediately, the smell of smoke, concessions, and a faint whiff of

something both sweet and putrid—the corn syrup factory—
fills the car.

Jamie shrugs, studying a new text message. "Me too, I
guess," she murmurs, reaching absently for a puffy blue coat
at her feet.

Maren giggles as she gets out of the car, pointing to a sign
affixed to a reflective white pole. "If you see something, say
something," she intones seriously. "Like what? Blood?" She
points at the front of Taylor's sweatshirt and laughs then
shrieks, "I see something!"

The Thicket entrance is marked by a wall of stacked,
house-high hay bales bridged by a dimly lit banner to form an
entry tunnel into the main plaza. With the flurry of new snow,
the ground is a little muddy. Already, the parking lot is
turning a little soupy from all the foot traffic.

As they reach the path to the entrance, Taylor can see fire
barrels blazing in the distance and the ticket trailer. The kids
standing in line look like shadows, backlit from the sparking
orange fire barrels.

As they stride toward the strobing lights ahead of them,
footsteps fall in unison on the damp ground, Maren grabs
Jamie's arm and giggles. "Wait a second. *Now* I see
something. Check out that guy."

Jamie and Taylor follow Maren's line of sight to an older
kid wearing a bunny costume and rabbit ears. He's walking
toward the end of the line, flanked by two boys dressed as
mediocre vampires. And he's holding what appears to be a
bunch of real carrots in one hand.

Taylor stifles a laugh. "Of all the costumes out there, he
chose that?" she whispers incredulously.

Jamie is trying to hold back laughter so hard she's starting to shake. "Is he going to eat those tonight? Like, are they a snack or . . ." She trails off, earning her a snort from Maren.

As they approach the end of the ticket line, the rabbit turns around to give Maren and Jamie an appraising look. Beside him, one of the vampires lets out a low wolf-whistle.

Maren lets her coat fall slightly off one shoulder. She gives all three boys a coy smile as she pushes her chest out and moves a little closer. Then she slowly shakes her head back and forth as she points at each one of the boys in turn. "Nope, nope, and nope."

Jamie tries to match Maren's ice-queen poker face but can only manage half a second before she crumples against Taylor with a squeaky honk, shaking with laughter. The rabbit looks at Maren like he's debating whether to use the B-word or the C-word, but ultimately he goes with a classy "asshole" under his breath. He turns around and shuffles a few feet forward in line, still clutching his bunch of carrots.

Maren shrugs and pulls her coat snug around her chest again, squinting into the tall, bright spotlights surrounding the ticket trailer. The spotlights are a new addition, positioned like four small suns above a metal detector and table at the front of the line.

A guard wearing a tan collared shirt and heavy black coat, his brass badge blazing white in the halogen glow of the spotlights, is positioned next to the metal detector. He's taking his time emptying the contents of purses, directing kids to reveal the insides of their coat pockets, and collecting masks from the kids who have clearly been living under a rock for the past several weeks. Only after this laborious process are the kids allowed to walk to the trailer window to purchase their admission.

The line isn't quite as long as Maisie warned, but Taylor still guesses they'll have at least a thirty or forty-minute wait to get into the plaza. She shivers and pulls her sweatshirt and coat around her more closely, hoping all the fake blood has dried by now.

"Holy crap, look!" Jamie squeals suddenly, pointing and practically jumping up and down. The rabbit ahead of them glances over his shoulder at her with a look on his face that says he isn't afraid to pull out the real insults now. When he realizes that Jamie is motioning toward the front of the line—not at him—he looks relieved.

Taylor gasps. She sees it too. Approaching the metal detector in the distance is a short, skinny kid wearing a beak mask.

Maren sees it now as well. She laughs out loud, standing on her toes for a clear view. "Oh my god. Are you kidding me? I wish we had some popcorn right now."

Before the kid in the beak mask can even make it to the metal detector, the security guard is on him.

The front of the line is still too far away to make the conversation that ensues audible. But from the way the guard is gesturing, hands flung out to his sides, thick frame towering over the kid in the mask, it's not hard to guess what he's saying. For a second, it looks like the guard has decided to escort the kid into the plaza—maybe to call his parents? Maybe to jail?

Taylor isn't sure what the protocol is here. But when the kid takes off the mask it's clear, even from here, that he's crying. Actually crying.

The security guard runs a hand over his mouth, shaking his head in exasperation and letting his hands fall to his sides. After a moment, he holds out a hand and takes the black beaked mask, striding over to the table and dumping it into a rain barrel next to the metal detector.

An enormous sign stating NO MASKS, visible even from here, is taped to the black barrel.

"That was freaking amazing," Maren breathes. They watch in silence to see if the kid makes it through the metal detector once he reaches the ticket window.

He does, cowering in front of the guard as he slips through. And then the ticket line resumes its low rumble of chatter and shuffling along the dirt and gravel path.

"That was nuts," Taylor exclaims to Maren, taking a couple of steps as the line inches forward.

Jamie, who has unhooked her arm from around Taylor's waist, doesn't move forward with them.

When Taylor turns around, she sees Jamie's face lit blue from the screen of her phone. She is texting furiously, a look of panic in her wide green eyes.

Maren sees it too and takes a step back in the line. "James. Earth to James. What's up?"

Jamie doesn't look up from her phone. She just shakes her head quickly.

When Maren tries to grab the phone, Jamie takes a step back and nearly collides with two girls in line behind them.

Her jaw tenses, but she still doesn't look up. "Nothing, okay? Just leave me alone."

Maren's glossy purple lips twist into a frown. '

Taylor grabs Maren's arm, sending her a meaningful look. Then she says, "Jamie? Stop texting for just a sec and tell us what happened, okay?"

Jamie stares at the phone a moment longer then suddenly shoves it deep in her coat pocket. Taylor can't tell if she's about to cry or explode.

Ahead of them in line, there is another ripple through the crowd and a few gasps. Taylor peers around the staggered queue of kids to see what everyone is looking at now. This time it's a girl with spiky black hair who's getting the third degree. The security guard holds her purse in one hand, gesturing toward the line of kids with the other.

It's still too far away to hear what they're saying or what the guard is holding for that matter. Taylor turns back to Jamie but reaches a hand inside her purse to make sure there's nothing that could be construed as a weapon in there. Chapstick. Gum. Keys. Tampons.

"Just—tell me if I'm, like, overreacting," Jamie blurts out. Her eyes narrow as if she is already anticipating their response. "Russ just texted me a photo from Maisie's party. He's *already* there. And guess who's hanging all over his shoulder, boobs practically in his *lap*?"

Maren shakes her head and frowns. "The angel."

Jamie nods. She's shaking slightly. "He *knows* I can't even stand her. Is he, like, trying to make me feel bad for not going to the party with him tonight? I already said we'd stop by later. Is he messing with me? Like, what the hell?"

Taylor loops her arm through Jamie's, pulling her closer and taking a few steps in line. "What did you text back to him?"

Jamie falters and takes a shaky breath. "I—I just said, 'what the hell?' And then he acted like he didn't know what my problem was. And then I sort of blacked out and told him that he's an asshole," she adds miserably. "Was that too harsh—I mean, given the circumstances? Crap, maybe I am overreacting." She looks stricken and pulls her phone back out of her pocket. "I'm going to apologize."

Jamie hesitates, looking at the photo on the screen then handing it around. "But just *look* at that. Does that look like a photo of somebody with a freakin' girlfriend?" She buries her head in Taylor's shoulder and groans.

Maren is still shaking her head. "Tell him you're not going to Maisie's party anymore."

Jamie lifts her head from Taylor's shoulder and looks at Maren, startled. "What? But we already—"

Maren gently takes Jamie's phone and puts it in her own pocket. "It's simple, James. If he's trying to mess with you, he's not worth your time. And if he legit doesn't understand that he's messing with you—even after what you just texted him—the last thing he deserves is a sexy devil in his lap too."

Maren pauses to glower at the rabbit, who is clearly eavesdropping on their conversation. Then she angles herself away from him and continues. "That angel skank doesn't hold a candle to you, James. I mean, for one thing, her forehead is *massive*. Like, Elliot-Stabler-from-*SVU* massive. Where does it even end? And I'm sorry, but there's a very fine line between classy cleavage and desperate cleavage. Know how to work it, bitch."

Jamie's furrowed brow relaxes slightly. "Right?" She studies the photo Russ texted again. "That's a wardrobe malfunction just waiting to happen." She unconsciously adjusts the strap of her devil costume and looks at her phone in Maren's hand. "Taylor, what should I do?"

Taylor shakes her head and smiles. "You shouldn't be asking me. The only boy texting me right now is my dad." She says this last part a little louder than she'd intended—which means the rabbit looks over his shoulder again. She pretends not to notice and continues. "Maybe just put your phone away for a little bit, and let's go stuff our faces with caramel apples and mini donuts?"

Maren nods solemnly then adds loudly, "So that when we shit our pants from fear in the Thicket, it'll be an extra good show." She cuts her eyes toward the eavesdropping rabbit and laughs.

Jamie's furrowed brow relaxes as she bursts out in high-pitched peals of laughter and shakes her head. "Ew. You're so gross, Maren."

Taylor giggles too. "Not what I had in mind. But probably gonna happen. Let's just relax, have a good time, and forget about Russ for a while? Maisie's party will still be going on when we're done here . . . if we still wanna go."

Maren reaches inside her coat pocket to pull out a large blue water bottle. "So . . . I was going to save this for later, but Sergeant McSearchy up there seems to be extra dedicated to his job." She nods toward the front of the line, where yet another mask is being confiscated. "And now seems like the right time anyway."

Jamie and Taylor look at each other in confusion. "You want to . . . get hydrated?" Taylor asks.

Maren laughs and unscrews the cap to the bottle. "Yep. I wanna get *real* hydrated. As hydrated as possible."

As she opens the bottle, Taylor catches a whiff of something sharp and acrid. "Maren!" she whispers in what she hopes comes out as mock shock instead of actual shock. "Oh my gosh. Where did you even get that?"

Maren shrugs. "It's not like my parents lock it up. And it's not like we haven't had a drink before now."

Taylor considers this. It's technically true. At a sleepover a couple months earlier at Jamie's house, they'd smuggled a beer out of the fridge while Jamie's mom was at her hot yoga class. They each took turns taking small sips while they waited for the water to boil for the macaroni and cheese.

Taylor is surprised when Jamie reaches for the bottle gratefully. "Bless you, Mare." She tilts the water bottle back and takes a long swig, making a face. "That needs a chaser so bad," she chokes out in a whisper. "It's called a chaser, right?" Taylor can smell the acrid sharpness on her breath now.

Maren laughs and takes the bottle from Jamie, throwing back at least a shot without flinching. Then she offers the bottle to Taylor.

Jamie looks on expectantly. So Taylor reluctantly takes the bottle and swallows a bigger gulp than she'd intended—as if it really were water. It tastes like nail polish remover, and she can feel it burning all the way down her throat, settling in her empty stomach like lava.

She gasps and coughs while Maren makes a show of whacking her on the back as the rabbit turns around in line yet again. "Went down the wrong tube," Maren says loudly, holding up the half-empty bottle. "Nothing to see here, Bugs."

Jamie giggles gleefully and takes another sip of vodka. "Hurry, let's finish it before we get any closer to the guard," she whispers as they creep forward in line. Taylor can see the security guard's face more clearly now. He's younger than she thought initially, with a patchy red beard on a patchier ruddy face. He has thinning brown hair under his hat and is wearing an expression that says he's not messing around here.

Taylor nods and takes a second—smaller—swig of the bottle. It's not as bad as the first one, and she manages not to make a face.

"Atta girl," Maren says, nudging her and taking another drink from the bottle.

By the time the water bottle is empty, they're only a dozen people away from the metal detector. As they huddle at the last fire barrel, Maren turns and tosses the water bottle into a trash can a few feet away. She laughs out loud when it bounces off the side and into the grass with a plastic *thwack*. "Nothing but net."

Jamie giggles and stumbles against Taylor, who is starting to feel a trickle of dread beneath her growing buzz. Will the security guard be able to tell that they're drunk? Will he make them leave? Will he call her dad?

"Guys, act sober," Taylor whispers urgently, nodding toward the guard and wiping the smile off her face. "Just until we get inside."

Maren stands up straight and salutes her, "Yes sir. Yes zombie ma'am, I—"

Jamie interrupts with another snort of laughter. "You guys, look." She gestures to the front of the line again.

Taylor sees who she's pointing at. A girl wearing an enormous pair of sweatpants and a thick hoodie. The sweatpants are so big that the security guard is making her turn her pants pockets inside out.

"Is that a costume?" Maren says, shaking with laughter and grabbing Taylor's arm. "Oh my god." She steps forward in line and pokes the rabbit in the back. "If so, it might be worse than yours, Bugs!"

The rabbit, for once, ignores her. Maren shrugs it off, turning back to watch the girl in the sweatpants. "I would literally die if anyone saw me wearing pants that big."

Taylor laughs too, but as she watches the girl tuck her pockets back into her sweats, she realizes she's wearing almost the same outfit.

CHAPTER 25

He waited to get in line until the girl with the purple wig appeared. She couldn't seem to stop touching the two vampires who fell in line beside her. She batted her long, sparkly false eyelashes, which had been applied a little crookedly, while she flirted and giggled.

She was carrying a conservative but decent-sized purse—nothing security would worry about. It had purple flowers embroidered along the soft knit surface that just matched her hair. And the zipper is already open a few inches.

He gets in line behind the girl and the vampires. And then he waits for the right moment.

Ten minutes later, a commotion up front at the mental detectors captures the crowd's interest. As the line moves a few feet forward collectively and everyone cranes their neck to see, he takes a larger step than he needs to. Then one hand moves to the knit purse as he gently jostling her other arm.

She even doesn't notice. Or turn around. And he doesn't apologize. Instead, he deftly slips the knife out of his coat and drops it inside her half-zipped purse.

The ticket line is only a little longer than it was fifteen minutes earlier. But it is significantly denser. Everyone has packed together more tightly. The thrill-seekers are anxious—but not necessarily impatient—to get inside. The periodic scenes at the metal detector provide ample entertainment as a pre-show. And the steady drip of adrenaline, the anticipation of the wait, is half the fun. The anticipation is only building. In his veins most of all.

When the girl with the purple hair reaches the front of the line, she tosses her purse onto the table casually, oblivious to the quiet thunk. Then she pulls her coat pockets inside out and patiently in front of the haggard-looking rent-a-cop with the tan hat who is frisking her vampire friends.

The rent-a-cop checks the girl's pockets and nods for her to join her friends on the other side of the metal detector while he searches the knit purse with the purple flowers.

After a few seconds, the rummaging stops.

The rent-a-cop slides the zipper fully open, leaning down just slightly, to confirm what he's found without lifting it out of the purse.

Then he pivots on his heel to look at the girl with the purple wig, who has turned away from him, whispering something to one of the vampires.

In one swift motion, the guard buries the knife in the barrel with the rest of the contraband he's confiscated. He does it quickly, before anyone waiting in line sees it.

Unlike the other contraband busts of masks and black lights, he doesn't yell. Although his face turns the same shade of red. It's impossible to hear what he's saying, but it's painfully easy to read the expression on the girl's face. Confusion. Then panic. Then horror and desperation.

Paul Blart is clearly ready to kick her out of the Thicket— maybe even call a real cop. But as he jabs a finger at the parking lot, she starts to cry. Big tears that streak her gaudy makeup and make her look more like a child than whatever sultry celebrity she's trying to impersonate.

The ticket line has gone impressively quiet, attuned to the fact that something interesting is happening at the front. The girl blubbers loudly now, swearing up and down that it isn't hers. That she's never seen it before. That someone must be playing a prank on her. She glances accusingly at the two vampires in her party, who hold up their hands as if they are being held at gunpoint. Their mouths are frozen in small Os of disbelief.

The security guard's expression says that he might be willing to let her through just to make her shut up. She hasn't said the word *knife* yet. But she's getting louder. More hysterical.

Finally, he relents, leaning close to her ear and placing the purse back in her hands while she nods dramatically, snuffling and wiping at the tears that are still coursing down her cheeks. She glancing fretfully at the kids in line behind her who stare in horror and fascination.

When the rent-a-cop finally steps back, the girl ducks her head and hurries away from him, toward the darkness of the plaza and the thumping rhythm of the DJ booth.

The two vampires trail after her. And then the line moves forward, the incident all but forgotten.

When it's his turn, he pays for his ticket in cash and allows the red-faced guard to inspect his coat pockets and turns his pants pockets inside out before he steps through the metal detector.

Squeaky clean. Not even a cursory glance at the thick fleece sweatshirt he's wearing that's been lined with coils of thin kevlar rope, or the innocuous plastic pen that casts a faint blue-white light when you click the top, or the latex gloves beneath the wool mittens on his hands.

He smiles as he walks through the looming corridor of hay bales then into the dark melee of the main plaza. With each step, he can feel the coil of the kevlar winding across his stomach and back in small loops. He's not surprised it worked. But he is pleased

When he's safely ensconced in darkness, he turns around to look back at the brightly lit ticketing area where the front half of the line is visible. His gaze settles on the table beside the metal detector. The bin of contraband is filling up rapidly.

He allows the pulse he's been reining in to rise just a little.

CHAPTER 26

To Taylor's relief, she's standing inside the main plaza.

The security guard with the patchy beard failed to notice how long it took her to successfully unzip her coat. And when he checked her pockets, he made no indication that he could smell the vodka on her breath—although she could certainly smell his. Taco Bell, if she had to guess.

Even Maren had been waved through without more than a terse warning that the ribs in the skeleton costume's corset might set off the metal detector. They didn't. Although Maren had offered to take the corset off if necessary, earning her a thin smile and a hat tip from the guard.

Now that they're past the security station and the ruddy-faced, sour-breathed guard, Taylor feels the alcohol warm her all the way down to her toes.

The snow is spitting tiny flakes again, and she sticks out her tongue in a clumsy effort to catch some. Grabbing Jamie's arm to keep her balance, she tilts her head back toward the swirling white dots that are just visible in the flashes of flickering light from the DJ booth.

Taylor closes her eyes and breathes in. The sweet, slightly putrid smell of the corn syrup factory has been edged out by a melange of hot oil and sugar, along with something dark and earthy. It smells like Halloween, she decides.

The sound of calliope music floats through the darkness, and when she opens her eyes she sees an enormous, wheeled Jack-in-the-box emerging from the shadows. The box trundles toward them along a wide dirt trail. The lid is open a few inches.

When the box comes within a few feet of them, Maren steps directly in front of it, her hands on her hips. "Let's see it," she slurs, twirling her wrist in the air and stumbling over to peer beneath the lid.

The box stops, and so does the calliope music. The lid closes completely.

Maren laughs and reaches out, presumably to pry the lid open. But before she can touch it, the box explodes with a deafening scream and a shower of blood and guts.

Taylor shrieks and Maren leaps to the side, tumbling into Jamie.

The calliope music starts up again as the box trundles forward. Taylor realizes that the blood and guts are actually confetti, streamers, and beads in different shades of red.

It's basically an enormous party popper.

"That was freaking amazing," Maren exclaims, hugging Jamie, who is still trying to catch her breath.

They continue toward the strobing lights of the DJ booth. Already the music is so loud that it's hard to hear much else— besides the intermittent screams. The phrase "Severed heads," is repeating in a monotone voice, beneath the thumping bass rhythm of a heartbeat.

Taylor startles again as a clown wearing a camo jumpsuit leaps out from behind a blind of dry corn stalks. He manages to surprise a cluster of teenage boys huddled around a fire barrel. One of the boys is so startled that he spills the bag of popcorn he's holding. The clown fist-pumps the air in a slow spiral as he slinks back into the blind of corn.

Taylor grins, realizing that she's been steeling herself for a preschool version of the Thicket. After all the protests and the talk of "new safety precautions," she was worried the scares would be watered down.

Thankfully, the Thicket is still solidly PG-13. She keeps her eyes on the thin tuft of orange hair that is just visible between the thick stalks of corn as the clown waits for the next group of kids to congregate around the fire barrel.

They hit the food trucks first, loading up on corn dogs, caramel apples, french fries, lemonade, and a family pack of fresh mini donuts drizzled in caramel and bacon bits. They eat their stash while they wait in yet another food vendor line.

There's plenty to keep them entertained while they wait. A full production of "Thriller" starts up every twenty minutes on the lawn near the DJ booth. And the plaza is crawling with scarers intent on sneaking up on unsuspecting kids in the darkness. Usually, some of the scarers are local kids who agreed to this gig for free in exchange for extra credit in senior drama. The program has been suspended this year.

Staked signposts direct thrill-seekers toward the different attractions across the plaza. There's a kiddie maze that gets a meager amount of use on weekends, an enormous corn maze on the other side of the plaza, a long row of "corn cannons" where you can shoot ears of corn at zombie mannequins, and a fortune-telling tent behind the ticket trailer.

But none of these lesser attractions draw much attention.

The tide of dark figures in the plaza are either in line for food vendors or drifting steadily toward the entrance to the wooded trails.

The line for the old corn syrup cabins snakes along the inside wall of the plaza and through switchback after switchback of cordoned ropes and hay bales staggered with more large "If you see something, say something" signs.

It's going to be at least an hour's wait from the time they get in line for the cabin trails. Taylor can't even see the end of the line from here.

Scarers dressed as bug-eyed clowns, ax murderers, and other boogeymen weave in and out of the cordoned ropes, popping out of the darkness near the fire barrels and skulking between hay bales.

As the girls approach the end of the line, Taylor spots a security guard holding a radio. The guard is leaning against the trunk of a limbless pine tree. Just in front of him, from somewhere within the line for the wooded trails, a chainsaw roars to life. A shrill chorus of screams cuts through the din in the plaza.

The line breaks apart, and a gruesome Jason wearing a dingy white hockey mask appears. He's chasing a thin blond girl who has angry red slash-marks across her face. Presumably, the girl is an actress.

The security guard doesn't look up from his radio.

"Better-than-sex french fries, better-than-sex donuts, better-than-sex corn dogs." Maren ticks off the loot as she takes a bite of each food and sighs happily, ignoring the chainsaw performance and neatly stepping through a wide break in the line.

The coat that was wrapped tight around her shoulders earlier is now halfway unzipped to carry her share of the food. She's wedged the stick of the corn dog into the cleavage at the top of her corset, with the caramel apple in one hand and a cardboard container of french fries stuffed in the inner pocket of her coat.

Jamie looks thoughtful as she finishes chewing a bite of caramel apple. "You know, you're so right. Why does everyone talk about sex so much, anyway? Like, it was *fine,* but it wasn't as good as this food." She grins and takes another bite of a caramel apple.

Taylor nods like she knows, reining in a smile as she watches Maren's obvious internal struggle to stop herself from making a comment about "lovemaking."

Taylor is a little surprised that Jamie hasn't asked for her phone back yet. Whether it's the lingering buzz from the alcohol, Maren's pep talk, or the enormous pack of mini donuts tucked under one arm, Jamie is smiling again. Taylor secretly wonders—maybe hopes—that this might be the end of Russ and Jamie. He's nice enough, as high school boys go. But she far prefers single Jamie—and single Maren, for that matter.

As they get to the end of the line, Maren focuses her attention on trying to take a bite of the corn dog that's still wedged into her corset. When she finally succeeds, Taylor and Jamie cheer.

"Hey, baby—can I have a bite?"

The voice comes from further up the line. Taylor feels her senses struggle to rally beneath the warm fog of the vodka buzz. Her gaze settles on a boy with his back to a fire barrel in line. He's about seventeen, she'd guess, but it's hard to tell with the black stubble he's painted across his chin. The boy cranes his neck to get a good look at Maren, who has paused her efforts to take another bite of the corn dog. However, she hasn't removed it from her cleavage.

Taylor rolls her eyes and glances at Jamie who, to her surprise, is running her fingers through her long, auburn hair and laughing. Jamie squeezes closer to Maren so that she's in the boy's line of sight too.

Taylor squints at the boy again. He's reasonably good-looking, she decides. He's supposed to be some kind of lumberjack, wearing a plaid shirt and holding a fake ax. Paul Bunyan, maybe. But she can tell that it's the way he's standing that has earned him reciprocal attention from Maren and Jamie. He looks casual, confident, his arms at his sides instead of stuffed into his pockets. And he isn't snickering with his friends like the bunny from earlier. Instead, he's looking at Maren intently as if he actually expects her to invite him over for a bite of corndog.

Maren leaves the end of the line and walks toward him. She gets just close enough that she has a clear view of where he's standing with his friends.

She glances back at Taylor and Jamie with a raised eyebrow. And then, satisfied that she doesn't see any major protests to what she's clearly about to do, she unzips her coat just a little further and flashes a smile. "Trade you a bite for cuts in line?" she calls to him.

There's a swift reaction from the people directly behind the boys in line. One girl, who is dressed as a kitten, makes a huffing noise and turns to glare at them. Her friend pipes up, "No cuts allowed, ho."

Maren ignores it. And so does the boy with the black stubble, who smiles. He gives her—then Taylor, then Jamie—a once-over. His three friends, who have been occupied with pulling handfuls of hay from one of the bales, perk up and look now too.

Jamie giggles. "You can have some of my donuts!" she yells hopefully and nudges Taylor, who holds up a half-eaten caramel apple with a shrug. She's not that anxious to cut in line. Or share their night with anyone else.

But the boys are already waving them up—to the annoyance of the rest of the line.

"Um, I really don't think you can do this," says the kitten, who is standing with her arms crossed behind the cluster of boys. The girl links arms with her friend and steps forward, as if to block their path. But at the same time, a scarer dressed as a zombie lurches from behind a trash barrel just behind them. The girls turn around and scream—while Taylor, Jamie, and Maren slide beneath the cordoned rope.

"Thank god. I'm so bored of lines," Maren slurs loudly, reaching for Taylor's elbow to steady herself as she stands upright. At the last moment she shifts away from Taylor and reaches for the flannel sleeve of the boy with the black-painted stubble. "Show me the blooooood," she trills.

Still holding the boy's sleeve, Maren stands on her tiptoes and looks past him to see the entrance to the cabin trails, which is still maybe a thirty-minute wait. "I'm Maren," she says, plucking the corn dog out of her cleavage and handing it to the boy before he can ask. "This is Taylor and Jamie. What school are you from?"

"Raft River," the boy responds, accepting the half-eaten corn dog and taking a big bite. "I'm Aaron," he adds with his mouth full. "This is Tyson, Ben, and Ryan."

Taylor sighs as Jamie leans toward the boy on the left—Tyson—who has thin, too-long wisps of peach fuzz on his upper lip but is built like an Abercrombie and Fitch model.

"Mare, give me my phone back," Jamie calls playfully as she tugs on the back of Maren's coat. She sidles closer to Tyson to offer him a mini donut.

Taylor understands what will happen now: Jamie hasn't actually forgotten about Russ—she's just found her own angel. Metaphorically speaking.

Maren pulls the wrapper off her caramel apple. Then she zips her coat up just far enough that her corset disappears behind the puffy fabric but leaves her boobs still visible. "I'm cold," she whines, ignoring Jamie's request. "Why is it so much work to be sexy?" She grins as she stumbles a little closer to the boy with the painted black stubble—Aaron. He reaches out to grab her arm as he takes another enormous bite to finish the corn dog.

Taylor sneaks a glance at the two remaining boys: Ben and Ryan. Both smile at her halfheartedly. Neither is wearing a costume. "Nice hair," says the shorter one—Ryan—who has muddy brown hair and freckles. "Are you, like, a garbage pail kid or something?" His grin widens like he's just said something clever.

The other boy—Ben—who is tall, blond, and a little too skinny to pass muster with Maren or Jamie but is cute enough —rolls his eyes. "She's a zombie, dumbass." He smiles at Taylor. "That blood is sick. It looks totally real." He's wearing an oversized gray Raft River hoodie and jeans, his hands shoved deep into his pockets.

Taylor flashes Ben a noncommittal smile and feels an elbow in her side as Maren suddenly lurches back in her direction. Maren's breath is hot and her whisper is too loud in Taylor's ear when she hisses, "There's two of them. Be a sexy zombie."

Taylor sighs and pushes Maren away. She's not sure how to interpret the advice. "Be a sexy zombie, there's two of them," as in, *make them both fall in love with your walking dead self?* Or as in, *stop being such a wet blanket, you have two options for goodness' sake.*

Either way, she decides she's still buzzed enough to go along with it. As long as everyone else is, anyway. Taylor turns back to Ben. "Thanks. It *is* real," she says with a straight face, feeling a flush of pleasure when she earns a genuine laugh in response.

Unsure what to say next, Taylor cranes her neck to see the front of the line. She watches as a small cluster of girls is allowed past the gatekeeper, a tall, thickset man with a black hood and long scythe.

The gatekeeper keeps the scythe crossed in front of the narrow entryway to the trails for around five minutes between each group of kids. She can't see his face behind the oversized black hood. To his left, a staff member dressed as a mummy stalks toward the kids who are coming up on deck to enter the trails.

"Hey, you guys, look!" Maren suddenly belts out loudly, pointing. "It's Sweatpants."

Maren points to a spot in line maybe a dozen yards away and a few switchbacks to the right. It's the girl from earlier, the one with the giant hoodie and sweatpants.

The girl looks up quickly then just as quickly looks away. Taylor isn't sure whether she actually heard what Maren said or just noticed the drunk girl gesturing loudly in line.

The boy with the black stubble—Aaron—scans the crowd where Maren is pointing. "Who's 'Sweatpants'?"

Maren waves her arm in the girl's direction again, and Taylor cringes. "That girl. Do you think she's dressing up as something?" Maren laughs and taps on a sign staked in the hay bale beside them. She affects a sweet, singsong voice: "If you see something, say something—like a crime against fashion."

The line around them, including the kitten and her friend, erupts in giggles. Cuts have apparently been forgiven in lieu of the free entertainment.

Taylor shifts on the balls of her feet and steals another glance behind her in line. The girl is turned away from them. And she doesn't appear to be listening, thank god. They're only a dozen yards away from the gatekeeper now.

Taylor smiles at Ben again, unsure what else to talk about but warming up to the idea of holding onto his arm while they walk through the cabins. She can be a sexy zombie. The sky isn't spitting snow anymore, but the temperature is still dropping. He's a warm body, at least. She grins to herself at the zombie joke, wishing she could tell Maren.

Tyson casually wraps an arm around Jamie, who is shivering noticeably. She smiles at him, and Taylor wonders if she'd kiss him with that mustache. It's really long.

As the line shuffles forward, the freckle-faced kid with the brown hair, Ryan, clears his throat. Until now, he has been standing behind the rest of them, kicking at the muddy grass.

"You know, Aaron actually knew the kid that got killed. He knew his sister."

Maren and Taylor turn around to look at him, leaning forward eagerly "Are you serious?" Maren asks. "We knew her in, like, middle school. She still goes to our high school. Idaho is so freaking small."

Aaron shrugs, clearly pleased with the reaction and the sudden rapt attention. "We hung out a few times. She actually told me that her brother was a total dick. She was texting me the night it happened."

Maren freezes as she plucks a handful of cotton candy from within her coat. Her eyes go wide. "Are you serious? She was *there* that night? Tell us everything."

Aaron looks thoughtful, the black stubble marks stark on his pale face. "I think she was supposed to be hanging out with him. He was, like, harassing the staff and being a huge pain in the ass. So she went back to the plaza and left him on the trail."

"What the hell?"

The voice is quiet, but it stops Aaron mid-sentence. His face goes even whiter, and Taylor thinks she sees a flash of recognition in his expression.

The girl wearing the sweatpants has left her spot in line and is standing directly behind them along the blue cordoned rope.

"Seriously. What the *hell* is wrong with you. You don't know what you're talking about."

Maren's mouth drops open when the girl calls him by name—or maybe it's the f-word.

Taylor feels her hands go suddenly numb with dread inside her sweatshirt pocket as she fervently wishes she were anywhere but here right now.

Because Taylor recognizes the girl too.

It's Norah.

She's not wearing makeup. Her eyes, which are usually lined in a thick layer of dark shadow, look pink and naked. And the wisps of dark brown hair that are visible underneath the hood of her jacket look lifeless and greasy. She's almost unrecognizable.

Norah has her fists balled up at her sides, and her gaze is fixed on Aaron in a death glare. "He wasn't a dick. He was just a little bit different. I don't care what I said. You don't know anything about him. So shut up."

Out of the corner of her eye, Taylor watches the gatekeeper at the entrance to the trails shift slightly. She wonders if he can hear what's going on—and if he'll intervene.

Norah stops talking and clamps her mouth shut tightly as if trying to hold the rest back. Her lip quivers slightly. Her gaze shifts to Maren. Then Taylor and Jamie. Her eyes widen with recognition. "Fuck you guys too," she whispers.

The slick feeling of panic in Taylor's stomach turns to dread. Why is Norah here right now? What's happening?

"I'm sorry," Aaron mumbles. "I didn't mean—"

But Norah is already walking away, her hands balled in tight fists as she pulls the strings on her hoodie tighter.

"Bitch," Maren says lightly, zipping her coat back up to her chin. "What was that? How the hell did she know all that stuff anyway?"

Taylor shakes her head, still feeling nauseated. "She's not a bitch. That was *Norah*." She glances at Aaron, who is still watching Norah walk away with a stricken look on his face.

Maren's mouth drops open. "No *way*. That was *her*? Without the eyeliner . . ." She trails off. Aaron has removed his arm from around Maren's waist.

The line around them has fallen silent, and Taylor can feel her cheeks burning. For a few moments, nobody says anything.

Maren shifts and looks in the other direction. The line creeps a little closer to the man in the black hood. They're only four groups away from being admitted now. But all Taylor wants to do is go home.

She studies the dark shapes milling through the plaza, trickling toward the cabins. Why is Norah here of all places? Taylor knows it's impossible, but part of her really believes that her own guilt manifested Norah here against her will.

Jamie finally breaks the awkward silence, offering her mini donuts around. Aaron and Ryan smile feebly and take some. Ben shakes his head and looks down.

The line around them begins to murmur, then laugh again, as everyone gears up for the cabins.

Maren slides an arm around the back of Aaron's plaid shirt with a sultry smile.

A lump remains stuck in Taylor's throat. Until right now, Norah Lewis was a ghost from her past. But everything feels different now. Heavier.

Taylor swallows hard, shaking her head and telling herself that the night can still be salvaged. She wasn't the one laughing about Brandon Lewis. And Norah has surely heard worse things by this point.

As the group in front of them walks through the entrance to the cabins, met by a snarling devil that makes even the hooded figure blocking the entrance jump, she almost believes it.

CHAPTER 27

While he waits, his gaze settles on a group of teens near the front of the line for the cabins.

The girls are drunk, he determines.

He studies them with interest as the one in the black and purple corset tries to twerk against a fire barrel. She nearly lights her short blond hair on fire in the process.

The girl shrieks and falls against the tall boy with the painted black stubble.

The redhead in the devil costume is laughing so hard she can't seem to catch her breath.

The brunette dressed as a zombie is still staring after the girl in the sweatpants who stalked out of line to confront the group a moment ago.

The blond in the corset is yelling something. The boys are laughing. The line widens around them as the other thrill-seekers exchange irritated and amused glances.

He's found the fringes of the herd.

He's here to hunt, after all.

CHAPTER 28

The wind whips through the dusty plaza, blurring Norah's vision. As she walks away from the winding line and back through the murky main plaza, she wonders whether Aaron and the girls are still following her with their eyes. Or if they have already forgotten.

She hadn't planned on seeing anyone she knew tonight. And if she did see someone, she definitely hadn't planned on confronting them.

Batshit crazy.

Norah realizes her hands are shaking, and she shoves them harder into the pockets of her enormous, ugly hoodie. *Stupid. So stupid.* But even as she berates herself, her high makes it hard to remember exactly what they said.

He told them that you were at the Thicket that night, the mocking voice cuts through her buzz. *Aaron told them that you left your brother alone. Which you did. Where's the lie?*

Norah clenches her fists and shoves the words into the black hole.

As she approaches the plaza exit, she stops and sits down on a hay bale, swiping at her face until she can see again. Until the fuzzy blanket inside her mind wrap her up again.

She can't see the end of the line for the cabins anymore. In front of her to the right is a dirty white tent, zipped shut on both. To her left there is a mini-donut stand where a few kids are waiting in line, glancing anxiously in the direction of the main attraction.

Norah tilts her head to look up at the sky, studying the stars that prickle brightly against the moonless, inky blackness. The wind has picked up significantly. She wonders, while she watches the white freckles of light wink and fade, how the wind could possibly make them twinkle in the airless vacuum of space.

When her hands are calm, she takes a steadying breath and swipes at the cold, wet trails on her cheeks. She hadn't realized she was crying. As she tucks her hands back inside the warm pockets of the old hoodie and flexes her fingers, she feels a solid object in the side pocket. With a start, she remembers that she brought her cell phone with her. She pulls it out of the pocket and opens the screen to see if her mom has texted.

She has. *Dinner?* It was sent half an hour ago. Norah hits ERASE to make the message disappear and takes another breath.

She should leave. Really leave.

The smell of mini donuts popping in hot grease mixes with the sound of distant screams, the rapid-fire pop of the corn cannons, and the first notes of "Thriller."

Norah looks at the empty, black exit. Unlike the bustling entrance, the exit is just a gravel path flanking the edge of the cornfield and the parking lot. She feels a prickle of regret and looks back at the plaza. She was almost at the front of the line. If she goes back now, she'll have to wait another hour at least.

Norah stands up and cranes her neck to see if she can see the front of the line from here.

She can't. It's too far, and too dark. But she's certain that Aaron and the girls are gone. They were only a few groups away from the front of the line.

That kid was a total dick.

Norah presses her fingers against the plastic case of the cell phone in her pocket Then she pulls the phone out again to check the time. It's 7:30. She wonders what her mom decided to eat for dinner and whether she will call if Norah isn't home soon.

Letting her gaze wander back toward the plaza, she notices a man approaching the dirty white tent to her right.

The man is not out of place, exactly. Shadowy figures are milling around everywhere. But the slightest tilt of his head as he glances to the left, in the direction of the plaza, bothers Norah a little.

She squints, trying to make out his features through her blurry vision. Heavy coat. Slim figure. Silhouette of a beard. And while she can't see his face, she is suddenly sure that it's the same man she saw in line earlier. The one who was with the girl.

He deftly lifts one flap of the tent, slips underneath it, and is gone from view.

Norah stays sitting where she is a moment longer, brow furrowed, feeling her breath become shallower. Then she stands and takes a hesitant step toward the dingy canvas tent. Was he supposed to go in there? Should she tell someone?

Batshit crazy.

Norah has no real reason to be suspicious. She doesn't know who he is. Or what the white tent is.

Still, she remembers the slight tilt of his head. And she feels somehow sure that if he'd seen her watching, he would have walked in the other direction instead of ducking into the tent.

Norah looks around. She can't see any obvious staff members or security personnel from here. So she walks toward the dirty tent, pausing beside the flap where the man disappeared. There's a zippered door in the thick canvas material. And a cracked plastic sign that reads "Staff only."

She frowns. Maybe he's a staff member. But if that's the case, why was he standing in line earlier tonight?

Norah reaches out for the zipper then pulls her hand back. Keeping one eye on the entry flap, she turns and walks toward the mini-donut stand.

"Excuse me," Norah calls, waving a hand toward one of the employees. A somber-looking, deeply tanned boy who is filling a cup of lemonade from a bubbling fountain inside the brightly lit trailer turns around. "I just saw someone go inside that tent—I don't think he works here, though."

The employee glances past her, toward the tent. His expression doesn't change. "That's just where everyone changes costumes and stuff."

Norah can feel the lines in her forehead deepen. "Okay. He was acting kind of weird, though. Could you check?"

The kid's expression shifts from somber to annoyed. "I'm not supposed to leave the donut stand. There's a line." He nods toward the small group of kids surrounding the counter. Then he places a lid on the cup of lemonade and hands it to a redhead in a parka.

The redhead glances at Norah with a smirk.

"I'll let security know when I have a sec," he calls over his shoulder, turning his attention to the back wall of the stand. A shiny metal tube is popping tiny beige O's into a sizzling yellow river of grease along the wall.

Norah stays where she is a moment longer, feeling her stomach rumble despite herself as she watches a second employee drizzle maple and bacon bits onto a pile of hot donuts.

She looks back at the white tent. Then she slowly makes her way back to the bale of hay to think. A sign that says "If you see something, say something," is just visible, staked along the dirt path that leads back to the cabins.

She allows herself a hiccup of laughter. Then she pulls her cell phone out of her pocket and brings up the saved contact.

Officer Willis. Minidoka County Police Department. He was the officer who interviewed Norah the night it happened. And then again the day after. He left her his card. Told her to call, anytime if she thought of anything.

Norah grits her teeth and taps the number before she can think about it.

He picks up on the second ring. "Rupert Police. Officer Willis."

Norah clears her throat and summons her best calm, not-high voice. "Hi, Officer Willis. It's Norah."

There is a short pause, "Hi, Norah."

She's a little surprised he answered. She clears her throat. "I'm sorry to call you randomly, but I'm at the Thicket, and—"

He interrupts. "Hold on. You're at the Thicket right now?"

Norah glances at the canvas tent again and feels her cheeks suddenly get hot. The flap of the tent is still closed.

"Yeah. I just . . . I um. I wanted to see it before they . . . pack everything up."

She squeezes her eyes shut. She sounds like a moron. Even so, she rushes ahead. "But that's, uh, not why I'm calling. I was sitting down for a few minutes by the exit, and I saw someone go inside a tent."

She hurries to add, "I don't think he works here. I'm pretty sure I saw him in line earlier. He had a beard. I—I tried to tell one of the employees—just a kid working at one of the food stands. He said he would let security know, but I don't think he did."

Officer Willis doesn't answer right away. And Norah can feel the thread of the conversation slipping away from her in the silence on the line. A few cold pinpricks land on her bare hand as she holds the phone. It's snowing again.

When Officer Willis finally responds, his voice is softer. "Thanks for letting me know, Norah. I'm sure everything is okay. But I'll get a message to Dave just in case. He's head of security there, really a good guy. We used to work together." He pauses, and she's sure he's trying to find a graceful way to tell her to go back home. Or to ask if her parents know where she is right now. Instead, he adds, "I'm sure it's not easy being there right now, Norah. Glad you called."

To her horror, tears well in her eyes and something deeply broken alligator rolls in her chest. "Okay," she chokes out. Then she hangs up the phone.

Norah stays where she is a few moments longer, wiping her face with the sleeve of her hoodie. Then she stands up, tucks her hands back into her pockets.

She walks away from the white tent, retracing her steps through the plaza until she reaches the end of the line for the cabin trails.

CHAPTER 29

He can't believe how easy it is to find the knife.

He'd expected to sort through the contraband piles. The haphazard collection of debris is overflowing from two plastic bins on the folding table beside a long rack of costumes and props.

But as he walks toward the bins, he sees it. The knife is separated from the rabble, in a torn cardboard box on the end of the folding table. It's nestled beside two pocket knives, patiently waiting to be recovered.

He takes the hunting knife, leaving the smaller blades in the cardboard box. He's careful not to touch either one of them.

The tent smells just like he remembers. Musty latex and the nearly overpowering tang of sweat from unwashed costumes.

He scans the fraying tarp beneath his feet in the dark tent, looking for a break in the fabric. Then he crouches and uses his fingernails to pry up one of the long, steel tent stakes. Brushing the dirt from the rusty metal, he tucks it into his other pocket.

The white staff tent was a hive of activity during the two hours before opening. After closing, it was the same story. Staff members applying makeup and changing into or out of costumes, coordinating schedules, repairing props, swapping stories. However, the benign-looking tent was strategically set up far enough beyond the main plaza that staff and management rarely used it otherwise. The last thing anybody needed was kids poking their noses in the staff tent or getting a hold of the props and costumes.

The mini-fridge sits the corner like he remembers, perpetually unplugged and gathering dust. If he guesses correctly, there's one lukewarm, expired diet Coke in the back. The mini-fridge is a "luxury" none of the staff ever really got to enjoy. Once you were in costume and working the trails or the plaza, you weren't allowed to leave your post unless someone tapped you out. And once you were assigned a post for the night, you stayed put for the duration—usually a five-hour block—to minimize complicated staff swaps.

That's how all of it had worked five years ago, anyway.

He knew things might have changed. Especially with the new "security" protocols. But he'd gambled on human nature operating like normal.

The panicking parents and PTA moms wanted metal detectors, bag searches, and more rent-a-cops. More signs. More safety they could touch and see.

Nobody was looking at an old white staff tent.

Five years ago, the lost and found had been kept in the back of the costume tent. Contraband wasn't much of an issue then. There were no masks to confiscate, no bags to search, and no metal detectors.

Still, there had been one kid—dressed as Zorro—who had the audacity to bring a real sword to complete his costume.

That item had been quickly confiscated.

And stashed with the lost and found.

"Kids are so freaking dumb," Tim had said to him that night, in a rare moment of camaraderie after closing. "The kid with the sword probably still has to use safety scissors at school," he added as he changed out of his costume and back into his street clothes in the dim light of the glowing space heaters.

He nodded as Tim unbuttoned the collar of his white shirt. High and frilly, straight out of *The Crucible*. Perfect for hiding just how loosely—or tightly—the gallows rope wrapped around his neck. "What'll happen to the sword?"

Tim had shrugged. "Looks expensive, so I'm sure we'll hang onto it. Management probably called his parents."

He wonders if the boy's parents ever did retrieve the sword. For all he knows, it was packed up with the rest of the chaos in the tent a few days later, when Tim's white collar turned red.

He scans the two piles on the table, keeping his attention focused on the distant muted chaos outside the tent. He's reasonably confident that the guard who dumped the second bin of contraband here ten minutes earlier is likely to be the only visitor for at least another hour. And he's also reasonably confident that no one saw him walk inside. But even if they did, and even with the signs shouting "if you see something, say something," he knows they're unlikely to do more than shrug and turn back to their bag of popcorn.

He's learned not to skulk. The trick is confidence and calm.

Still, he has no interest in explaining what he's doing in the staff tent if he can avoid it.

There are numerous black lights in the bins of contraband. A diverse collection of masks. Two disposable cameras. And what looks like a set of nunchucks. He smiles slightly as his eyes land on a familiar black mask poking out from the middle of the pile.

He nudges it gingerly with the sleeve of his coat, bringing the black latex to the top of the pile.

Tenderly, he slips a finger through the dark eyeholes then pulls the mask into his jacket.

He'd considered bringing the original. But the logistics of planting a hunting knife and a mask weren't worth the effort.

This discovery feels like serendipity.

He feels his pulse speed up again, then carefully tamps it down.

After passing through the metal detector with flying colors, he got in line at the nearest food vendor. It was something to do while he waited for the bin of contraband to fill up. The girl with the purple wig and crocheted purse had stomped past him at one point, followed by her bewildered friends. "Seriously, how did it get in your purse?" one of them kept asking.

For a while, the girl with the purple wig had stood with her arms crossed tightly over her chest, just inside the ticketing area. Like she might decide to leave the Thicket of her own volition after all. She kept shaking her head at the two boys who appeared to be apologizing for god-knows-what. Certainly not planting the knife.

Finally, the girl had tossed her hands in the air and moved toward the food trucks, while the boys followed close behind.

If she'd been a boy, the security guard with the patchy red beard and the sour face probably would have called her parents. Maybe even the police—the real ones. But between the tears and the convincing pleas that she didn't know where the knife came from (along with an impressive amount of blubbering and smearing her too-thick mascara around her eyes while she gestured angrily at the two boys who held up their hands in protest) the guard had let her into the plaza anyway.

He scans the dark tent until he spots a familiar set of white plastic bins. In the first one, he finds what he's looking for underneath a first-aid kit: a few tubes of glue, some thin plastic sheeting, and several rolls of Gorilla tape.

He tucks the Gorilla tape into the deep pockets of his black coat along with the folded square of plastic sheeting.

The knife, the sheet, the tape, and the tent stake feel heavy and good in his pockets.

He considers rummaging through the rest of the bins, on the off chance that he finds something else he likes. But there's really no need.

He has what he needs.

As he exits the tent through the back flap that is visible from only one side of the plaza, he reminds himself not to look from side to side or rush too much. He calmly re-zips the tent flap and mentally rehearses what he will say if he is questioned. "Sorry, I was just looking for a bathroom," with a sheepish shrug and a smile. The line of port-a-potties isn't visible from this half of the Thicket.

As he walks across the plaza back toward the crowds, he spots a security guard headed toward one of the mini-donut stands. He keeps his eyes on the main plaza and doesn't speed up his gait.

The guard is leaning on the counter of the donut stand and talking to an employee, who gestures toward the tent.

Keeping one eye on the guard, he veers slightly toward a stand selling cotton candy and caramel apples.

The guard turns to look at the tent. Then he shakes his head and waits while the kid ladles a heap of mini donuts into a red and white cardboard tray.

Finally, the guard ambles toward the tent, adjusting his too-big hat before popping one of the tiny donuts into his mouth whole. A moment later, the guard unzips the canvas flap and disappears.

He tucks a hand into his pocket to touch the utility knife as he reaches the front of the cotton candy line. "What are you supposed to be?" the girl at the counter asks, eyeing his beard while he pulls a five-dollar bill out of his front pocket and requests a bottle of water. "That beard is sick. Is it real?" she asks.

He chuckles softly. He knows that between the thick beanie on his head and the beard, the only thing you can see clearly is his eyes. "Thanks. *Duck Dynasty*. You watch it?"

The girl shakes her head and turns to retrieve his bottled water. "Doesn't the beard get, like, food and stuff in it?"

He chuckles again. *Not food.*

He studies the tiny hairs on the nape of her neck as she reaches into the refrigerator for the bottle of water. The hairs are feathered like duck down, beneath her ponytail. That's where he would cut. The knife inside the coat pocket feels substantial and warm against his side.

By the time he has finished the transaction at the cotton candy booth, the security guard has re-emerged from the tent. As the man readjusts the ridiculous tan hat on top of his head, he lifts a hand and waves at the employee at the mini-donut stand. The employee, who has already gotten back to filling sodas, doesn't see.

The rent-a-cop shrugs and walks back toward the other side of the plaza.

CHAPTER 30

"You WILL hand it over right now, or you WILL be escorted out of the Thicket," Maren repeats in a deep, strained voice. Then she breaks out into laughter for the umpteenth time as they exit the last cabin, mimicking one of the guards. "Could they *be* any more anal?"

"Seriously. What a letdown," Jamie adds, laughing, her arm still tucked into the crook of Tyson's arm. "I mean, most of it was pretty good. But Cabin Twelve was gonna be, like, the *highlight*."

Taylor nods in agreement. Overall, she'd give the Thicket an A-minus. The effects, the staff, and the props were realistic, creative, and legitimately scary. And everyone—including the boys—had let loose at least one ear-splitting scream.

However, *the* cabin—the room where it actually happened—had mostly been a joke. Just a bottleneck of kids lingering at the entry and exit points. Everyone kept trying to sneak photos with their cell phones and flashing black lights that somehow made it through the bag search.

There were two guards in Cabin Twelve. One stood outside the door, and one stayed just inside of the room itself. Both guards had been tenuously costumed as part of the production itself, since the room had been reconfigured as a dingy jail cell. The guards' presence made the animatronic inmates, rattling their chains and flinging themselves at the cell bars, decidedly less scary. There wasn't much of a chance to let the eeriness of the room itself seep in.

Still, there had been a brief moment when the beam of a contraband flashlight suddenly illuminated the wall behind one of the prison cells. The soft purple glow had revealed a dim, glowing pattern of dots and splatters across the back wall and floor, behind the two inmates.

The pattern was faint. But it was everywhere.

Constellations of tiny white dots created haphazard patterns halfway up the rough logs. The dots dribbled into thin tails, like comets. And a thick, blotchy pool spread across the floor near the back wall of the cabin, disappearing out the door in a dribble.

The patterns reminded Taylor less of blood than of the glow-in-the-dark paint she'd tried to apply to her ceiling in elementary school. She remembered balancing on the edge of her bed in the dim light so she could see where to paint the tiny stars. While painting, she'd stepped forward without thinking—right off the edge of the bed, dropping the entire bottle of paint on the carpet. Despite several scrubs, the invisible splotch on the carpet still glowed faintly green-white in the dark. She'd given up on a ceiling full of stars after that, abandoning the tiny patch of constellations.

"Holy mother of—is that—" Ben had said when the splatter patterns suddenly appeared in the beam of the black light. Maren and Jamie turned around to look—but not before the flashlight clicked off. One of the guards strode across the room toward the source of the light, holding out his hand and booming, "You WILL hand that to me now, or you WILL be escorted out of the Thicket."

Taylor had taken a small step backward, her arm inadvertently brushing against Ben's. He had laced his fingers into hers with surprising confidence, and she left her hand in his as they exited Cabin Twelve.

Maren had regaled everyone with her loud imitation of the guard as they continued down the trails into the next nest of monsters. Jamie laughed harder each time, irritating the group of kids behind them so much that one kid, exasperated, finally yelled for her to shut up. Maren only repeated herself louder.

Taylor had snuck a glance down at her hand, still interlaced with Ben's, debating whether to lean in or pull back. She doggedly ignored Maren and Jamie's attempts to catch her eye. Ben wasn't really her type. But he wasn't *not* her type. She wondered if maybe he was trying to comfort her—after seeing the blood spatter.

Ironically, it was the flash of the black light in the crowded cabin that finally lifted the uneasy pall trailing Taylor since the confrontation with Norah Lewis. Suddenly, it felt like the awkward encounter had happened days ago. To someone else, maybe.

Taylor had squeezed Ben's hand back and let the tension evaporate into the cold, cloudless night. Then she laughed along with Jamie, exclaiming over the fake blood spurting from severed latex limbs in the next cabin. There was no use dwelling on the faint pattern on the walls in the cabin, or picturing Norah's crumpled face.

As they loiter near the exit to the cabin trails, Taylor studies the faces of the kids who emerge. They range from exhilarated to disappointed. Most of the kids are still talking about the constellations on the cabin wall. Whether they saw the blood or, in most cases, didn't see it. Whether it was so much blood or less blood than they'd imagined after all the hype. Whether it looked like the Thicket had tried to sand down the log walls. How much blood had been in the bathtub they'd removed from the room. Who got their black light taken away.

Taylor lets her gaze trail over each group, scanning beyond the exit to the hay wall bordering the plaza. She realizes she's still keeping an eye out for Norah. Did she go back home? Get back in line? Complain to the security guard? Is she crying in the parking lot now? There's no sign of her on this side of the plaza.

Taylor notices that her fingers, which are still laced in Ben's, are starting to feel clammy. She pushes the image of Norah's face away to focus on what Maren is saying.

"I mean, it would have been a *little* cool—if we saw the blood too." Maren turns and casts a pointed look at Taylor and Ben, leaning on Aaron's flannel chest. Aaron grins, his teeth flashing white against the black paint around his mouth. He grabs Maren's waist with one hand, letting his other arm dangle heavily across her chest.

Tyson glances at Aaron sideways. Then, his sparse blond mustache glimmering faintly in the strobe lights, he drapes his arm around Jamie.

Jamie grins and reaches into her coat pockets. Then she frowns. "Mare, do you still have my phone? I'm okay now." She looks up at Tyson while she says it, running her hands over his leather bomber jacket.

Maren smiles, still looking up at Aaron. "Nah. You two make a very cute couple, but you are not sending a selfie to Russ right now. Don't think about him again yet."

Jamie's mouth turns down in a mock pout, and Maren shakes her head. "You'll make Tyson feel bad." Maren turns toward Taylor, out of Jamie's line of sight. She flicks her finger along her upper lip, miming a mustache.

Tyson, who clearly does not feel bad—or sense that his mustache is being mocked—smiles and pulls Jamie against him. Jamie giggles and snuggles into him.

Ben clears his throat and shifts on his feet, squeezing Taylor's clammy hand tightly. "So, uh, what should we do now?" He nods toward the other end of the plaza. "You guys want more food?"

"Sure, we could—" Taylor begins. She's interrupted by Maren, who is already shaking her head.

"I'm still full. Let's do the corn maze next," Maren exclaims loudly. She spins around so she's facing Aaron.

Taylor tries not to look at Ben and keeps a neutral expression on her face. Maren has basically just announced that she wants to make out with Aaron in the corn.

Behind her, Ryan's freckle face looks pained. However, he's pretending to be absorbed with the task of propping up one of the "If you see something, say something" signs that has been kicked over just outside the exit to the cabins. Taylor feels a little bad for him. It's painfully obvious that he's the odd man out. Although that hasn't stopped him from sneaking obvious glances at Jamie and Maren's boobs every few minutes. "The corn maze is lame. It's not even haunted," he whines, abandoning the fallen sign. "Plus it's shaped like a candy corn or something stupid this year."

Maren laughs. "God that's lame. But who cares what it's shaped like? It's not like you can tell what shape it is while you're in the maze, anyway. It'll be fun." She twists her fingers through one of Aaron's belt loops and pulls him toward the other side of the plaza, motioning for everyone else to follow. "C'mon."

With a glance between them, Jamie and Tyson follow.

Ryan sighs and looks at Taylor and Ben. "Jesus. Are you guys going too?"

Taylor can feel her cheeks burning beneath the dried greasepaint and zombie blood. She looks at Ben for her cue, but he's already tugging gently on their clasped hands. "Come on, it'll be fine." He grins and punches Ryan in the shoulder. "We have to do the corn maze. To get our money's worth for the tickets."

Ryan ignores him, studying Taylor. "Okay, but you do realize I'm the third wheel in your little tricycle, right?"

Taylor laughs, enjoying pretending that she and Ben are a couple. But honestly, she's glad that Ryan is coming too. "Come on Ryan. Safety in numbers."

Ryan mumbles something else under his breath, but he follows them anyway as they move toward the other end of the plaza. Beyond the DJ booth and the strobing lights, Taylor can just see the dark silhouette of the massive cornfields, barely visible in relief against the deep navy sky.

CHAPTER 31

He doesn't have to wait long for them to emerge.

Through the smoky light cast by the ring of fire barrels at the trail exit, he watches as the teenagers grin at each other, exclaiming over what they saw—and didn't see—in the cabins.

They jostle against each other, all eagerness and anticipation for whatever else the night might bring.

The group lingers for a few moments then moves with purpose away from the congested trail exit. They walk past the last of the food stands, past the kiddie maze, past the forlorn tire swings and sandboxes filled with dried corn. Then they head toward the far inner wall of the plaza.

He feels the rightness of it as he follows them at a distance. When they reach the entrance to the corn maze, he stops and waits.

A bored-looking guard with a tan hat, black coat, curly gray hair, and deep crow's feet—he's surely too old to be a rent-a-cop—is sitting on a hay bale. All around him, the corn stalks are cut and trampled to form a wide entrance into the maze.

The old guy doesn't look up as the teens enter the maze through one of the three narrow passages.

A wooden sign is staked in the ground:

No throwing corn.

No eating corn.

No urinating in the corn.

The plague doctor looks back at the frenetic beams of lights cutting through the dark plaza, making him blink when they suddenly flash in this direction. He waits a few moments longer. Then he walks past the old man in uniform and into the maze, feeling his pupils dilate as the darkness swallows him whole.

CHAPTER 32

Norah studies the monsters while she waits in line—for the second time.

The line for the cabin trails has nearly doubled in size in the time it took her to walk across the plaza and back. The staff have cordoned off more switchbacks with rusty metal chains, making the entrance appear much closer than it actually is at any given time.

A few new scarers have been dispatched to keep the crowds from growing too restless in the long waits. And to her surprise, Norah finds that they provide the perfect distraction to keep her from hearing too much chatter while she stands in line, hunched deep into her hoodie.

The scarers work as a pack. One creature—Norah isn't really sure what it's supposed to be—approaches a group of kids, crawling on its belly over the now-frosty grass toward a fire barrel.

There's blood matted in the hair on the animal's muzzle, deep red against the long, curly white fur. On the top of its head are two horns that curl downward, extending nearly to its back. Maybe it's a goat, Norah thinks. Whatever it is, the animal begins to bellow when it reaches the line. Kids sandwiched deep in the switchbacks crane their necks to see, and kids near the fire barrel spin around to exclaim over how ugly it is.

Then, from the back of the line—where no one is looking except for the recently arrived newcomers who watch with glee—a man dressed in all black creeps forward. He's wearing a short red wig, and his face is painted in mottled red and white. His eyes are swallowed up by dark black patches. But it's his mouth that takes the cake. Norah can't tell if it's a mask or some kind of demented mouthguard. Dozens of long, wicked-looking needles protrude from his lips and down his chin, sending swaths of blood cascading down his mouth and onto his exposed throat.

Needle Mouth is carrying a chainsaw. And as the kids collectively turn to gawk at the goat creature making a ruckus on one side of the line, Needle Mouth creeps in closer, closer. Then he lifts the chainsaw over his head, turning the machine on and screaming.

The entire line erupts in shrieks and screams. Despite herself, Norah feels the barest smile creep across her face and an unexpected rush of tenderness. There's some gawky kid inside that mask. She can tell by the lanky set of his arms and the way he stands. Maybe he knew the staffer who died the same night as Brandon.

She swallows and looks back at the goat thing, which has nearly been swallowed up by the dark plaza as it scuttles away.

As the line shuffles forward a few feet, Norah's gaze moves back in the direction of the food trucks, the concessions stands, and the white canvas tent. She can't see anything from here. But that doesn't stop her from looking.

Nothing has happened, of course. No SWAT team. No flurry of security. The man in the army jacket and beard hasn't reappeared. And she feels certain that the only person Dave—head of security—might be watching out for is a teenage girl wearing enormous sweatpants and tiny naked mole eyes. Her ears burn as she imagines the awkward conversation he and Officer Willis must have had. Respectful. Pitying. *Poor Norah.*

Norah's mom had texted her again, right as she took her place at the end of the long line for the second time. She had almost gotten out of line—again. It would be another hour, at least, until she made it to the front. But Norah stays where she is, watching for approaching monsters. She's grateful when they elicit the screams that stop the chatter about the cabins and the blood and the two people who died there.

She pulls out her phone and sends her mom a text. "Out. Home in a while." She watches the text bubbles pop up almost immediately after she sends it. They disappear, then pop up, then disappear again. Her phone informs her that she has 20 percent battery life. She ignores it, watching the text bubbles until they stop for good.

Norah feels a prickle of guilt as she pockets the phone. Her parents are good people. They're going through hell. They deserve better. But if what you got was what you deserved, Norah wouldn't be standing in line at the Thicket right now.

Another monster, a woman this time, staggers toward the line. She's dressed in torn scrubs covered with blood and entrails. One of her hands is full of enormous hypodermic needles. There's a stringy gray tangle of intestines hanging out of the elastic waistband of her pants, and her bare arms are covered in shiny red blood. "Does somebody need a doctor?" she shrieks, sending a portion of the line scrambling against the ropes. "Who needs a doctor?"

Me, Norah thinks. *Me.*

The line inches forward, and Norah balls her hands harder into her pockets until the sting of her fingernails on her palms helps her take a few more steps.

CHAPTER 33

This is where the real ghosts are, Taylor thinks as they round the first corner of the maze and the darkness envelops them.

The corn maze isn't quiet, exactly. The dry corn stalks rasp in the breeze, a constant chatter. And when the wind picks up, rushing through the mostly empty arteries of the maze, the stalks clash together in a loud rattle.

When the wind lets up, Taylor can hear crunching footsteps, giggles, and faint screams coming from further inside the maze. There's also the music from the DJ booth—along with the familiar, competing bass of "Thriller" thumping steadily through the night air. However, for the first time since they arrived, the crowds have basically disappeared.

Taylor glances over her shoulder for a last glimpse at the security guard stationed on some stacked hay bales just inside the entrance to the corn maze.

He's older than most of the other security guards she's seen. Late sixties, maybe. She wonders whether the corn maze is the coveted position or the bum job at the Thicket. There's not much to do here, sitting on the outskirts of the plaza in the dark. She tries to recall the expression on the man's face. He barely glanced up from the radio set in his hand. He'd looked a little bored but not necessarily unhappy.

Maren and Jamie—arm candy in tow—are leading the way through the corn maze. The girls are walking faster than before, still slurring their words even though Taylor's buzz is all but gone. She wonders how long it will be before the couples disappear down dead-ends.

"If we take every left turn, we won't get lost," Ryan calls helpfully from behind them, swearing softly when one of his shoes gets stuck in the mud—again.

The ground is uneven, strewn with half-broken stalks and partially empty ears of corn. The trail is thick with copious amounts of mud, despite the frigid temperatures and the spitting snow. The mess of leaves and cornstalks underfoot must be the reason. Every few minutes, there is a soupy, sucking sound and a laughing curse as someone steps into a hidden mud puddle.

Maren slows down and turns to look at Ryan with a sultry smile. In the darkness, her deep purple lips are stark in her pale face. She holds the smile for a moment then flicks her gaze to Aaron and darts into the maze, to the right.

Jamie giggles and tugs Peach Fuzz to the left.

Ryan swears again under his breath but keeps going, moving faster to keep up as Maren and Aaron disappear.

When Taylor and Ben reach the fork in the maze, they hear voices. A girl wearing a long red cape and hood suddenly appears, holding the hem of her garment up around her waist to keep it clean. "This is gross. And it's not even scary," she says to the boy beside her, pointing at her muddy red shoes in disgust. "I can't believe you left me back there. I was yelling your name."

The boy shrugs. "I couldn't hear you. It's freaking loud in here with the wind."

The girl in the red cape wrinkles her nose and flicks a glance at Taylor. "Fair warning: The maze is not worth it."

The boy, who has his face painted like a wolf, sighs loudly. "It's not that muddy once you get past the part everyone's been trampling over."

The couple's voices fade quickly as they continue walking, and Taylor hears Ben laugh softly beside her. "Wimps. I like it out here. It's kind of peaceful." She can feel him looking at her and is glad—again—that she's wearing face paint.

Just ahead of them, Ryan reappears in the darkness. "Are they both gone?" he mutters. Taylor squints into the maze and suddenly realizes that she can no longer see either Maren or Jamie—or anyone else—ahead of them.

Ryan groans and stops walking, using half a corn cob to wipe at the mud on his shoes without success. "I'm going back to the plaza, okay? You guys just . . . go do your thing. I'll go to the fortune teller's booth or something," he says half-heartedly.

Ben lets go of Taylor's hand and strides over to where Ryan is standing, looking miserable with the muddy corn cob in his hand. "Look, man. I didn't want to say anything in front of the others, but me and Taylor were kind of hoping . . ." Ben runs one finger suggestively down Ryan's jacket.

Taylor lets out a snort as Ryan shrieks and bats Ben's hand away. "That's freaking disgusting." One side of his mouth lifts in a reluctant grin as he glances at Taylor. "I mean, not because of you, Taylor. Just *him*." He shakes the corn cob at Ben. "Find me when you're done bumping and grinding, okay?" He shakes his head and walks past them, tossing the corn cob down a dead-end and peering in the direction they just came from. It can't be more than a five-minute walk through the maze until he reaches the plaza.

Ben laughs and takes Taylor's hand as Ryan disappears into the darkness and the whipping stalks that absorb the sound of his footsteps.

Taylor's pulse speeds up as she and Ben continue walking. What happens next?

When the wind dies for just a moment, she hears someone scream—then laugh. It might have been Jamie.

Taylor listens intently as the wind picks up again, but it's impossible to tell which direction the screams came from. She takes a few steps toward the next turn, avoiding looking at Ben, although she's still holding his hand. Ironically, now that the threesome has dissolved, she feels suddenly shy again, her heartbeat thumping hard in her ears.

Ben gently tugs on her hand, pulling her toward him along a wall of corn. His face looms dangerously close to her own. She can just see the dark pinpricks of stubble on his chin.

Trying for a flirtatious giggle—which comes out as a whinny—Taylor flashes a smile at him, unlaces her hand from his, and then sprints around the next bend in the maze. She hopes the gesture came off as playful. But she is suddenly worried she might pass out. What if he has bad breath? What if *she* has bad breath? She remembers the French fries she ate earlier and runs her tongue along her teeth. As she stops running, she notices absently that the boy they saw earlier was right. The mud really isn't as bad out here, with the ground less torn up from so many boot and sneaker prints.

"Hey," Ben calls softly behind her as he hurries to catch up.

Taylor hesitates as she stares into the darkness of the forking paths in front of her. Somewhere in the maze, someone screams again. This scream lasts longer. It's loud enough to cut through the rasping sound of the wind through the stalks, and it sounds further away.

"We can just go back if you want," Ben adds after a few seconds when she doesn't respond or turn around. "I'm kind of hungry anyway."

She can hear the disappointment in his voice—instead of the annoyance she expected. It endears him to her in a way she doesn't expect. She finds herself smiling, her pulse slowing a little. She can't feel the buzz from the alcohol anymore, but the fact that she drank it at all earlier in the evening still makes her feel reckless.

Keeping one eye on the fork in the maze in case Maren or Jamie appear, Taylor takes his hand again. Making out with Ben has to be better than standing around in the plaza with Ryan, waiting for Jamie and Maren to come out arm-in-arm with Tyson and Aaron. She already knows that the ride home will be spent in a play-by-play of the corn maze—not the cabins, or the flash of black light after all.

Taylor slides closer to him, running her tongue over her front teeth again and hoping he can't see it in the dark. She holds up the sleeve of her thick gray hoodie. "I'm sort of a mess . . . I don't want to get blood on you."

He grins, and she's relieved to see that his teeth look decently clean and white. "I'm not worried about it."

She grins back but glances away, listening to the wind whip through the corn around them. They're in a wider corridor of the maze. But every few feet, smaller paths straggle off like arteries, most of them dead-ending in a wall of cornstalks. Taylor wonders if Ryan has managed to find his way out of the maze by now.

They make their way down one of the artery paths, stopping when they hit a wall of corn.

Gathering her courage, channeling Maren, and praying that her lips don't taste like French fries, Taylor runs a hand down the front of Ben's jacket. She doesn't pull away when he reaches for her waist and gently brushes his lips to hers.

Somewhere from within the maze, or maybe the sound is coming from the distant trails and cabins, she hears more screams as the wind dips and swells. But all she can focus on is trying to tilt her head just right and move her mouth to match his.

CHAPTER 34

"Make sure you don't let her get too close to your brain," Ryan mumbles, trying to keep one eye on the damp ground to avoid mud puddles.

He smiles, impressed with his own wit. Then he says it a little louder, in the voice he wishes he would have used as he walked away from Ben and Zombie Girl. "Don't let her get too close to your brain."

Ryan stops as a sudden dead-end of thick stalks appears in front of him. This part of the maze doesn't look familiar. But then it wouldn't. The bitch with the skeleton costume and the smokin' boobs *wanted* to get them lost. If they had taken every left turn like he'd said in the first place, he wouldn't be stuck in this godforsaken maze by himself, in the dark.

He tries to visualize the candy corn shape the maze is supposed to be this year, calling up the image he saw on a poster at the ticket booth. He knows it won't help, but he does it anyway. The tip of the candy corn was at the beginning of the maze where they'd passed the security guard. Then the maze widened. Thirty acres at its widest point, the flier had said. Sixty acres total. How big was that?

A few yards to his right, along a different branch of the maze, he thinks he hears crunching footsteps. Since he left the group—or what remained of it—he hasn't seen anyone else. And it's pretty obvious why. After the cabins, the maze is about as fun as a wet rag. Unless you had the opportunity to get to second base with a sexy skeleton or devil. Which he didn't.

The wind picks up, obscuring the sound of footsteps. Ryan sighs, standing on his toes while he tries to see through the dark stalks. All he can make out from here is the shuddering, shifting haze of light to the west from the strobe lights in the plaza.

They'd gone further into the maze than he'd realized, and he feels a tiny bubble of fear that he might still be finding his way out of here by the time everyone else is finished making out.

A chorus of screams carries in the wind from further away, and he turns back in the direction he just came. He walks quickly toward the screams before they're swallowed up.

To his right, there is another scream. This one is close, shrill, staccato. He stops again, realizing he is breathing harder than necessary. *It's just dark,* he tells himself. Then he listens again for signs that anyone else is nearby—so he can follow them back out to the plaza.

There is nobody.

Ryan digs his hands deeper into his jacket pockets, wishing he had listened when his dad suggested a coat instead of a hoodie. He hadn't anticipated staying for the corn maze after the cabins. He hates the corn maze. It's boring. Corn and more corn. And in the dark, you can't even see the corn. Or anything else.

A muffled crunching sound comes from nearby. Was it a footstep? Something else? He squints through the stalks, but he still can't see anything or anybody.

He briefly considers yelling Ben's name. Or Tyson's. And he feels his face get hot even considering it. Not only is he the only one here without a girl now, but he can't find his way out of the stupid maze.

He's a complete loser.

The next scream he hears—coming from within the maze, he thinks anyway—is long and low-pitched. The sound takes a few seconds to fade away as the wind momentarily dies to a breeze.

He can't help but think about the murdered kid. Brandon. What did his screams sound like that night? Were different from these screams, or about the same?

Ryan shudders involuntarily and zips his hoodie all the way up to his neck.

Some of the kids who went through the trails that night— the night Brandon and the staffer died—went to Raft River High, in Albion. One kid in his math class claims he actually saw Brandon, facedown in the cabin.

Some people speculated that Brandon was still alive at that point. Barely, but still. It was hard to say.

There are more crunching noises, so close that Ryan is sure he should be able to see somebody by now. He clears his throat. "Hey?" he calls, narrowly avoiding a puddle of muck in front of him as he retraces his steps to a fork in the path then peers to the right.

Ryan feels more than sees that he is looking in the wrong direction for the source of the noise. The air feels suddenly heavier behind him.

It takes a moment for him to see the person standing in the middle of the path, even though he's just a few feet away. And it takes another moment for the reason to register.

There's no pale skin glowing faintly in the dark. No facial features materialize. There is only deep black.

The person is wearing a mask.

Ryan can feel his heart beat harder as the details of the mask take shape, slowly at first, then more quickly as the adrenaline kicks in.

The mask curves outward, into a smooth beak. It's one of the plague doctor masks.

The person hasn't moved at all.

It's a joke. Ryan runs the words slowly through his mind as if that will make them true. Some loser got past the security table and is playing a sick prank. Or maybe it's Ben, he thinks suddenly, wondering if Aaron and Tyson are in on the prank. Who managed to get the mask inside the Thicket?

But even as he tells himself why he shouldn't be afraid, the fear sends roots from the pit of his stomach down to his feet, holding him where he stands. He is aware of a loud, pulsing hum coming from within his own head, filling his ears with a rising roar.

The frame of the shoulders on the person wearing the mask is wrong for a kid. The build is too tall, too stout. It's not a high schooler inside the dark coat or behind the thick, black beak. If this a prank, it's not funny.

Ryan tells himself to move his feet. To run. But his legs feel leaden. He is rooted in the mud like the dead corn stalks.

His mouth moves, but all that comes out is a hoarse whisper in the back of his throat. Even if he runs, where will he go?

In circles.

Toward endless dead-ends.

In the dark.

The person wearing the mask moves for the first time, and Ryan's eyes follow the black hand as it reaches inside the coat.

The knife isn't extremely long. He can just barely see the glint of the blade as the man holds it upright in one hand then beckons with the other.

The gesture isn't threatening. Not yet.

The voice rises above the wind, but just barely. It's soft. Lilting, almost. "You can scream if you want. Maybe just once, for fun?"

And so he does, as if permission was all he needed. Ragged. And loud. Somewhere in the back of his mind, he thinks, *It sounds just like the other screams.*

The man wearing the beak mask takes a step forward. "That's enough. If you do it again, I'll stick this in your eye."

CHAPTER 35

If the boy had known how close they were to the gravel road just beyond the five-foot wall of corn, he might have run.

He wouldn't have made it far. Not with the mud and the dark and the uneven ground.

But he might have tried.

Instead, the skinny kid with the stark brown freckles in his sallow face follows him through the thin outer maze—an access pathway made every year for employees.

The outer maze is a throwback to the Thicket's early days, when the maze was haunted and easy access to the labyrinth of twisting paths and causeways was necessary for the employees to do their jobs. The outer maze made it possible to pop out of blind alleys and dead-ends draped in duck blinds and blood.

The creators of the maze still built it into the design every year, for convenience. Kids inevitably got lost. There were always four hidden "entrances" to the depths of the maze, one at each corner of the enormous cornfield. The outer maze was the first thing they built when the mini backhoes and graders arrived each fall.

The outer maze isn't shown on the Thicket's fliers, of course. This year's candy corn shape with the callout boasting "60 acres!" is just a triangular tangle of arteries. And the outer maze isn't readily accessible from any of the pathways that snake through the labyrinth of the maze itself.

You had to know what you were looking for. Where to push aside the thick stalks that appeared to be just another living wall.

He'd learned about the outer maze during orientation the year he worked here. And the narrow pathway still had its uses.

The kid with the freckles keeps up a reasonable pace. He doesn't stop. Or scream again. Not after the knife-in-the-eye comment.

But he won't stay docile. The same thing happens with mice when there's nowhere left to run. They go limp, frozen, heartbeat still frantically pumping beneath a cat's paw. Playing dead works. You wait for the predator to relax just a little, to ease up, to get bored. To bring the kittens over for a turn. That's when the mouse erupts in a burst of pent-up adrenaline. One last play for freedom.

Sometimes it works on the cats. Because cats are stupid.

He keeps an arm's length between himself and the boy, eyes moving steadily between the boy's head and the boy's hands. He stays close enough to easily grab the boy if he runs but not close enough to be taken by surprise if the boy suddenly whirls around, arms pinwheeling and fingers clawing.

It's maybe a ten-minute walk before they reach the right spot in the outer maze.

He can hear a group of kids walking through the inner maze. And from the slight tilt of his head, the boy hears it too. There are two or three kids, by the sound of it. Laughing. Talking companionably.

He steps closer to the kid with the freckles and lets him feel the knife at the base of his neck. Hard enough to hurt. Not hard enough to draw blood or elicit a whimper. Then he whispers, "If you scream, I will cut your windpipe out. Slowly. And they'll just run away."

He can see the kid's heartbeat through the pale skin at his throat, hammering hard.

The kid stays quiet. And after a few seconds, the group has disappeared back into the rasping stalks of the maze.

"Push through there, where the stalks are bent," he instructs calmly, waiting while the kid hesitates in confusion. The boy winces as he makes eye contact, like he's been burned. "It opens up on the other side." the plague doctor explains patiently. "Go through the stalks. Now."

He waits, while the kid tentatively parts a handful of stalks and steps forward, wedging his body between the thick corn stalks that reluctantly give way then swish back into place with a dry rattle.

As the boy takes another step through the corn, he follows. And after just a few feet, they've breached the outer wall of the maze. A narrow gravel road runs alongside this outer wall. It's big enough for a tractor or four-wheeler. But not a vehicle.

A few yards away, on a dirt knoll, are the black outlines of an old riding lawn mower and a mini backhoe. Long, haphazard rows of thick sprinkler piping crisscross the uneven ground. Further down the gravel path are two camper trailers. Judging from the grime and rust on the doors he inspected earlier, neither have been touched in months.

On the other side of the gravel road are cornfields and more cornfields. These fields, however, aren't cut into mazes.

Most of the cornstalks are broken, some trampled completely by Wind River's corn harvesters, which have already been through for the season.

To the right, in a weedy, half-cleared patch of dirt just behind one of the trailers, is a tall wooden building.

The old mill.

He prods the kid forward until they are standing even with the first trailer. Silhouetted against the darkness, a long wooden beam juts out from the top of the ancient building. Beneath the beam is a small, dark square opening in the frame of the building.

He smiles. That's where the piano wire fed through, attached to the back of Tim's pants on a hidden harness.

Or that's how the trick was intended to work, anyway.

There's not even a fence around the tall, dark edifice anymore. Just a halfway unreadable "No Trespassing" sign affixed to the outer door, and another one attached to the rickety hangman's platform.

They'd closed off access to the old mill, also after Tim's "accident" five years ago. That's when they had rerouted the maze and sold that portion of land back to Wind River. It had all been in the news. And a cursory real estate investigation showed that this portion of the land was no longer part of the lease to the Thicket.

As they reach the side of the small building, he watches the boy's muscles tense. If he puts up a fight, it'll be here. While he's free.

The boy turns to look at him again in the darkness, his eyes black and wide. "I'll do whatever you want, I don't care.

Just . . . please don't hurt me." The last part comes out thin and squeaky, like a deflating balloon.

Instead of replying, he tilts his head just a little. After a moment, the boy fully deflates and holds his hands out, quivering palms up, in the universal language of submission.

He's taking his chances with good behavior instead of mounting a fight.

The plague doctor almost laughs. It's a stupid decision. But it'll be easier this way. He smiles and points to the latch that is nearly hidden on the wall of the building.

The kid fumbles with and then opens the broken latch. He doesn't even have to prod the boy to step into the dark building.

The inside of the old mill smells of both dust and mold. As he pulls the door shut behind himself, he reaches into his back pocket and retrieves a penlight. The beam casts a thin, dim circle of light onto the floor in front of them.

The uneven wood floor is still covered in a thick layer of sawdust. It was something management thought up to add an authentic touch to the old mill. And to hide the copious amounts of mice droppings that appeared each morning, distracting customers from the gallows act and resulting in a complaint to the health and welfare department in Rupert.

He clears a space for a square of plastic sheeting, carefully moving a few broken benches that remain from years ago. Then he points to the sheeting and marvels as the kid walks onto it obediently, allowing his hands and legs to be carefully tied with the thin yellow kevlar rope and wrapped in layer after layer of Gorilla tape.

The boy's ludicrous hope—that maybe things aren't as bad as they seem—flitting just beneath his terrified expression is almost endearing.

It's fascinating, that denial. It stays until the very end for most people. If they don't fight, they freeze. And if they don't shut down, they hold onto hope. Always so much hope. Even bound hand and foot on a sheet of plastic in a dark building, by a stranger wearing a mask.

He uses half a roll of Gorilla tape on the boy's arms and legs. Fear makes people creative. You had to plan for overkill, then a little beyond it. When the rope is secured, he cuts a section from one of the arms of the thick fleece sweatshirt he's wearing and stuffs a piece into the kid's mouth. Then he wraps another section of tape around the boy's head, starting with the mouth but skipping the nose and eyes.

"Scream," he instructs, standing back to inspect his work.

When the kid squirms around, grunting a little instead, he kneels down and places the knife right above the boy's ear canal. He presses down just enough to draw a tiny blossom of blood.

The boy's eyes roll back into his head, and he screams in earnest, fighting against the tight bindings. But his efforts result in little more than a shuddering twitch that registers as a slight crinkle on the sheet of plastic.

He thinks of the legless fly. So much bound energy, with nowhere to go.

He closes his eyes and evaluates the scream. It comes out as a muted, impotent sound through the boy's nose. The sound is not necessarily quiet. But it's nothing compared to the wind and the real chaos in the Thicket, just outside the door.

He watches the boy a few moments longer, until he turns his head to the side and lowers it onto the plastic sheeting.

Then he walks to the door and shuts it carefully behind him, leaving the boy in darkness.

He stands motionless on the edge of the outer maze for a few moments, listening to the pale stalks whip in the wind. Feeling the icy pinpricks scattering snow. Breathing in the smoky, too-sweet stench of the corn syrup factory.

He closes his eyes, imagining himself as an animal.

A predator.

He removes the plague doctor mask and tucks it into the inner lining of his coat, keeping the knife in a zippered pocket.

A few moments later, he parts the barrier of corn concealing the outer maze and makes his way through the dense stalks and into the narrow causeway.

He waits a moment, focusing on the rhythm of his own steady breathing until he is sure that no one is close by.

Then he slips back into the main maze, hands tucked into his pockets.

As the wind ebbs and the stalks momentarily stop rasping, he hears a high peal of laughter in the distance.

He listens carefully, waiting for the wind to fall again.

Then he makes his way toward the sound.

CHAPTER 36

Ben's mouth, as it turns out, tastes like cologne.

Did he eat some of it by accident? Taylor wonders. Maybe it's just boy Chapstick. At least it isn't Taco Bell.

She pushes the thought out of her mind and tries to focus on the kissing tips Maren read aloud from *Seventeen* a couple of weeks ago. *Use your tongue sparingly.* Check. *Keep your eyes closed.* Check. *Get out of your head, stay in the moment.* Well . . .

To be honest, Ben is so into the make-out session that she's not sure he really notices what she's doing. She estimates that they've been kissing for about twenty minutes now. His hand has been making steady progress from her hip to the lower half of her rib cage. Five more minutes and they'll definitely be at second base. Or third. There's an ongoing argument about the bases between Jamie and Maren.

"Mmm," Ben sighs, sliding his hand up another inch, alarmingly close to the bottom of her bra strap underneath her sweatshirt. Taylor takes half a step back and he follows, pulling her toward him again. A layer of broken cornstalks scrapes across their jeans while the partially frozen mud gives a little beneath their feet with a slow sucking sound.

Her face makeup can't be in good shape. She opens her eyes a sliver, trying to see if any of the white and gray greasepaint has transferred to Ben's face. But all she can see is his up-close eyelashes and the skin between his eyebrows. She makes a mental note to stop at a gas station bathroom to wash her face before the drive back home.

As Ben's hand starts to roam again, Taylor takes a full step back, running into the wall of corn behind them with a loud crunching sound. There is gray and green greasepaint all over the lower half of Ben's face. A lot of it. She cringes and watches his expression fall.

"Uh, sorry. I thought you were into it," he says, shoving his hands into his pockets and looking down.

"Oh, um, I was," she lies. "*Am*. I'm just freezing. I stepped in a puddle of mud somewhere, and my foot is totally numb." That part isn't a lie. It's getting legitimately cold outside, even with a sweatshirt and coat. She can see faint puffs of air as she speaks into the darkness between them.

He looks wary but relieved, pulling her back toward him with one hand. "Gotcha. Do you want to—"

To their right, there is a small crash in the corn, followed by a flurry of pounding footsteps. Then silence.

They listen for a moment, but the sound doesn't come again. "Uh, okay." Ben shuffles his feet, digging into the muck at their feet with one foot. "Should we see if we can find our way back? Or—"

The sound comes again, above the wind. A flurry of breaking corn. Then silence.

From somewhere further away, there's a series of screams, and Taylor's stomach tightens. "Yeah," she whispers. "It's a little creepy out here. I can't believe we haven't seen—"

The sound of faint giggling floats through the air as the wind dies momentarily.

Taylor lets go of the breath she's been holding and motions for Ben to follow her. Then she quietly leads the way along the path, in the direction the giggle came from.

Sure enough, it's Jamie and Tyson. They're standing in a dead-end, two pathways over.

Taylor wonders if they've been there the whole time or if they've just wandered over from further inside the maze. She rolls her eyes.

Tyson's back is to them, and Jamie's face is just visible over his hunched shoulders. He's kissing her neck while she runs her hands up and down along his shoulder blades.

Ben holds a finger up to his lips and creeps toward them. When he's about a foot away, he lifts his hands in the air, crouches slightly, then pounces on Tyson's back with a loud yell.

Tyson windmills his arms backward and whirls around, nearly knocking Jamie over in the process. "What the *hell*—"

When he sees that it's Ben, he looks first relieved then annoyed. "Seriously, dude? Busy here." He casts a glance at Taylor. "You guys done already, huh?" He lifts an eyebrow and nods at Ben's now gray-and-white lips, glowing faintly in the dark.

Ben grins and turns toward Taylor with a shrug. "Come on. Let's get out of here."

As he takes her hand, there is an ear-splitting scream—and a crash—so close that both Taylor and Jamie yelp.

Beneath the steady rattle of the stalks, there's a distinct whimper. Then nothing.

It sounded like Maren.

Taylor looks at Jamie, who is already turning back toward Tyson. She glances toward Ben, who smiles reassuringly. Didn't anyone else hear it? "James, do you think that might have been Maren?" she asks.

Tyson tilts his head toward her and grins. "Probably. Aaron knows how to make a lady scream." He laughs, and Jamie joins in.

Taylor replays the scream in her head, trying to reach the same conclusion. Maybe it wasn't Maren. And even if it was, they were in a dark cornfield in the middle of the Thicket. Why wouldn't she scream?

No.

Maren likes to play it cool. At all costs, sometimes. She wouldn't scream like that over a scare—or a boy, for god's sake, whatever Tyson might think.

"Seriously, James. Will you come check with me? Make sure everything is okay?"

She feels an overwhelming sense of indignation as Tyson pulls Jamie slightly closer toward him—and Jamie lets him. Who does he think he is? They've known each other for all of twenty minutes.

Jamie turns her head toward Taylor, but even in the dark Taylor can tell that she's not meeting her eyes. "I really don't think that was Maren, Tay." With one hand, Jamie reaches to pull up her devil corset, which Taylor suddenly realizes is maybe three inches lower than it was the last time she saw Jamie. "Send her a text, ok?"

Taylor feels Ben squeeze her hand. "Come on, I'll look for her and Aaron with you. I'm sure everything's cool. There's lots of people screaming," he adds gently.

She lets him lead her away from Jamie and Tyson, already hearing the wet, slurping sounds of their lips—and heaven knows what else—before the sounds are swallowed up in the scratchy rattle of the corn.

Taylor listens intently, but the scream doesn't come again. Nothing that sounds like Maren, anyway. She can hear the drifting cries and shrieks coming in the direction of the plaza, and the cabins. But right now, the loudest noise is the stalks bending and dipping in the wind.

Taylor pulls out her phone, the blue-lit screen making her blink to focus. "Where RU? Corn maze is creepy. Hah." She adds a smiley face, still willing to keep it lighthearted.

She watches, just in case a string of bubbles appears below the text she just sent. Her battery has dipped from 70 percent to 40 in the past fifteen minutes, a little lower each time she checks her texts with the roaming drain in Declo.

Nothing.

A faint swishing sound comes from a few yards to the left, but when they walk in that direction, all they find is another wall of corn.

Ben squeezes her hand again as Taylor peers down a dark dead-end, hoping she'll see the back of Maren's neon purple skeleton ribs glowing faintly in the dark.

She doesn't.

And even though she knows that there's no real reason to worry—that it was probably just a scream—she suddenly feels very afraid.

CHAPTER 37

The girl with the black-and-purple corset had been a gamble. He'd seen the flicker of subversion in her eyes as he stepped closer, wagging the knife back and forth in front of her as she untangled herself from the kid with the painted-on stubble.

"Hell no," she'd muttered, turning fully around to face him, ready to fight. Ready to run from the black figure looming in front of her. The boy she was with looked between her and the knife as if she would give—or deny—permission to fight.

He'd stepped closer, backing her further into the dead-end while she hesitated. *Fight or flight.* Life or death.

She should have chosen flight.

As she lunged at him he had raised the knife, dragging it hard across her arm. He hadn't really wanted to cut her. Not yet. But she'd forced his hand.

She'd screamed of course. Half in pain, half in shock that the knife he was holding was real—and had just entered her skin.

He'd cut her straight down the shoulder, which was exposed in the open coat she was wearing, and down to the top of the heaving corset. No arteries.

And then, as he knew it would, the girl's expression had changed. The hope went out of it that maybe everything would still be okay or that this was some kind of joke her friends were playing. It was that unique teenage fable that carried some special adults into middle age. The one that led you to believe you were basically a character in a video game. That nothing could *really* hurt you.

That bubble of optimism disappeared quickly when something really did hurt you.

When she'd started to cry, her good arm pressed tight against the weeping blood that bloomed in a dark river over her exposed skin, he lifted the dripping knife and motioned to the path to their left. The outer maze was only a few yards away. "Shut up. And walk that way. Or I'll do that again but to your stomach this time."

The boy with the smeared stubble was still rooted to the ground where he stood. His eyes remained glued to the girl's arm. "You too. Unless you want me to gut her right here? Move."

And so they did. He still can't believe how easy it was to herd them. They moved silently and invisibly, like ghosts through the corn.

He finishes winding one last strip of Gorilla tape around the new boy's arms, already pulled tight behind his back with the kevlar. Then he pauses, dipping into his pocket to touch the three thin rectangles that have replaced the rolls of tape, weighing heavy in his coat. At his feet, the plastic sheeting shifts slightly as he stands up to inspect the three phones a second time.

Beneath him on the plastic, the boy with the black stubble and flannel shirt watches him with wide eyes in the dim penlight as the plague doctor presses the webbed, fractured glass of each phone's home button.

Nothing.

Satisfied, he tucks the three phones back into his pocket and kneels again to finish taping the new boy's legs. The dusty old mill feels alive again, filled with possibility. He can feel his pulse rise as he winds the Gorilla tape around and around, methodically weaving in and out on the bare skin at the ankles and calves, not the jeans.

The freckle-faced boy is lying in the sawdust an arm's length away, face upturned toward them even though it places his neck at an odd angle. He's taking fast shallow breaths through his exposed nostrils, and his pupils are wide and black as he stares into the middle distance.

His nose is making a whistling sound as the air rushes in and out. If he doesn't stop that soon, he'll pass out. Which would be fine. He'll wake right up.

The plague doctor inspects the new boy's legs, satisfied that they're secure. He notices that his own hands are trembling ever so slightly.

Three. This is more than he's ever had.

Tim was the first, of course.

The next time he'd done it, there were two. He'd taken a part-time job at a landfill the year after the temp gig at the Thicket. They'd made him a supervisor when he produced a resume he found online, citing managerial experience at a retail chain that had closed the year before. He always offered to take the night shifts, knowing that the right trespasser would come along eventually.

And they had. A man *and* a woman. There were drugs involved—evidenced by the quick shuffle of their hands and the looks of their teeth when he shined the flashlight on them in the dark. They'd come on foot. He could hear the trespassers who drove to the landfill gate and then snuck in from at least a mile away. These two were different though. They'd come on foot. He wondered how many times they'd met here, in the stink and the warm, rotting mountains of trash, to enjoy a few hits on a cold night. He'd guessed, correctly, that they were homeless.

He'd used a long section of rebar that time. First the man. Then the woman. It wasn't a particularly hands-on job. But watching them go under the compactor afterward had been interesting.

No one had ever shown up at the landfill to ask questions in the months that followed. There was no news coverage. No missing person's report. No police. It was like the couple had vanished. And he had done the vanishing.

He can feel the pulse in his neck now. He studies the new boy's face through the eyeholes in the tape, noticing the sheen of sweat and real stubble under the smear of black paint on his upper lip.

It's getting sweaty inside the beak mask too. So he takes it off, placing the mask on a dusty bench shoved against the perpendicular wall at a crooked angle in the rank sawdust.

The boy with the painted black stubble makes a low noise in his throat, thrashing a little on the tarp. He's louder than the freckle-faced boy, but not by much. The plague doctor leans down to inspect the wad of sweatshirt inside his mouth, forcing it in a little deeper.

The girl with the skeleton corset is lying in the sawdust on the opposite side of the tarp, a pool of red beneath one shoulder. When he turns toward her with the penlight, he sees that she is watching him—not her friends. Her nostrils flare above the Gorilla tape wrapped around her jaw, her expression cut in half but still readable.

She studies his bare face, and he sees the dissonance in her analysis. He knows he looks normal underneath the mask. Kind, even, in the right moment. Someone's dad or uncle.

He smiles at her and turns back around, enjoying the feel of her eyes on him as he double-checks the tape on the freckle-faced boy's legs. It *was* kind of him to bind her arms with just the Gorilla tape, instead of the rope. The fibers would dig right into the open flesh, sinking into the wound and increasing the bleeding.

When he glances up a moment later, it's the look in the freckle-faced boy's eyes that tips him off.

The boy isn't staring into the middle distance anymore. He's holding his breath now, neck craned even further, eyes fixed on a point behind him.

The plague doctor turns around just in time to see the girl with the black and purple corset launch herself at him, balancing precariously on her fused legs.

Her left arm—the one he cut earlier—is free, in front of her. A long strip of Gorilla tape dangles from it, whipping wildly as she lunges forward, struggling to stay upright. The whites of her wide eyes flash in the dim beam from the penlight.

The blood, he thinks, knowing he should have accounted for it. *Slippery bitch.*

He watches her fall before she even gets close to him, landing with a muffled thud at the edge of the plastic sheeting. But still, she manages to catch herself with her dripping free hand, landing hard on her hip, and somehow twisting to grab hold of a long, narrow piece of plywood half-buried in the dirt.

Fascinated, he watches. She's faster—and braver—than he initially gave her credit for, given her choice of costume.

Breathing heavily through her nose, she rolls onto her knees to face him, holding the plywood in front of her, still meeting his eyes.

The whole thing is so poorly executed, it's pitiable.

He stares at her for a moment. Her eyes are open wide, and she's making a sound deep in the back of her throat. The corset has twisted to the side, nearly exposing one breast. The purple ribs are jutting into the skin at her armpits.

He rises from where he is kneeling and takes a step toward her.

She grips the piece of wood—blunt, with a few splinters peeling off the ends—tighter in her red-stained fingers. As if she's in any position to harm him.

He retrieves the knife from the inner pocket of his coat. She coils back against her bound legs, ready to strike first.

Clucking his tongue, he reaches for the piece of plywood, grabbing the end with his gloved hands as she swings—hard, but not hard enough—at his head, then falling back onto her hip. In the penlight, he can see that the snowstorm of sawdust at her feet is turning a mottled red.

And then, of course, he does the only reasonable thing.

He kills her, firmly driving the blade of the knife beneath her chin.

There is a slick gurgling sound as she kicks at him for one, two, three seconds.

After that, she goes still.

He shakes his head and looks at the two boys. The freckle-faced boy lies motionless, his pinpoint pupils fixed on the sawdust, away from the blood. The other, the boy with the black stubble, is struggling against the ropes and the tape. Until the plague doctor walks closer. "Do you need something?" he asks gently, quietly. And then the struggle stops.

He looks down at his hands. Only a little blood. Not bad.

He wipes the blood onto his pants, inspecting the latex surface for rips or tears.

It's better this way, he decides. She was trouble from the start. And it will keep the other two quiet and still—for a while at least.

He is suddenly aware of voices, drifting from the direction of the maze.

He listens, waiting for the sound to come again as the wind crests then dips.

It's a girl's voice.

He looks at the two boys and cocks his head, listening. The sound comes again, faintly. Three drawn-out syllables. Someone is searching, he decides.

He looks at the boys.

He's hesitant to change his plans.

He'd be happy with three.

But if he finds another couple, there would be five.

He feels the familiar trickle of adrenalin pulse in the pit of his stomach as he touches the two remaining rolls of tape in his pocket, then carefully tucks the knife alongside them.

It's not too late.

And it will be easy enough.

As he walks back toward the outer maze, he stops to pull the three phones from his pocket. For good measure, he wipes the phones with a tissue from inside his coat. Then he tosses the destroyed phones into the middle of the narrow ditch just beyond the irrigation sprinklers with a quiet splash. The water isn't running anymore this late in the season, but the center is still a murky puddle.

They'll find the phones. Later.

As he enters the outer maze, he hears the girl's voice again, muddled by the rasping stalks inside the maze. As the sound disappears, he hears another voice. Lower, but not by much. A boy, this time.

He listens intently as he moves along the outer maze in the general direction of the calls, pausing while he waits for the sound to come again. *Marco.*

Head cocked, he peers down the long corridor of the outer maze. The wind swells, and when it dies he hears a shriek from the opposite direction. Then nothing.

It's getting late. Almost 9:00 now, by the position of the Big Dipper.

He considers this, then walks toward the eastern edge of the maze.

Despite the size of the maze, it only takes ten minutes to get from one edge to another—when you have the convenience of a straight shot through the outer maze anyway.

When he reaches the east corner, he can just see the bales of hay at the maze entrance, where a spotlight blazes at the edges of the dark, buzzing plaza.

The old guard is still there. He's still sitting down in the hay. It's impossible to make out the expression on his face, at this distance. But from the way he is stooped over his knees, he's either tired or bored. Probably both.

Satisfied, he turns back the way he came. As he walks, he listens, but he doesn't hear the boy or the girl calling anymore. Just the usual drifting screams as the wind cuts then rises.

When he sees the dark, narrow roof of the old mill in the distance, rising above the waving stalks, he feels the pull toward the secrets it contains. The pent-up, frenetic energy inside that makes him eager to get back.

Three. There's no need to force the numbers.

As he starts to walk back toward the mill, he hears a sudden peal of laughter.

It can't be more than a few yards away.

So he stops. Listens. And carefully makes his way toward the sound.

He's rewarded with a wet, slurping sound.

Kissing.

He feels inside his coat for the knife and touches the stickiness on the handle with the latex of his index finger.

Five.

CHAPTER 38

Norah wonders absently if she is going to pass out. But she keeps walking.

People stream past her in blurry waves, their faces featureless in the dark. She hears their shrieks and laughter as if she is floating underwater. Her vision has narrowed to a few pinhole pricks of light in scattered, snowy darkness.

She doesn't know where she's going. Just away. Out of the pulsing noise and flashing lights. Out of the crowd of shadowy shapes that brush past her.

Norah stumbles along the plaza wall, feeling the flannel lining of her hoodie catch against the bristly facade of hay. She walks until the strobing lights fade and the music isn't so loud.

When she can no longer feel the beat of the music pulsing in her ears, she stumbles toward a row of bales near the entrance to the corn maze, nearly missing her mark and tumbling to the side. She knows that people are probably watching her. They probably think she's high. And she is. But ironically, her high is the only thing keeping her from actually losing it right now.

She forces herself to take a breath. Flex her fingers. Close her eyes. Think about the breath moving in and out through her open mouth in smoky white puffs

It helps to sit down. But as the nausea fades and her breathing slows and steadies, an unexpected wave of grief breaks through the surface, making her gasp.

There had been no sign of Brandon in the cabin.

She'd known he wouldn't actually be there, of course. But she'd hoped, so deep down that she hadn't even admitted it to herself, that she might somehow *feel* him there. That a piece of the puzzle might click into place. That she'd see, somehow, that none of this had been her fault.

Anything. A sudden breath of cold air. A heaviness in the room. A sudden stillness.

She hadn't felt anything.

It was just a rowdy crowd. Just an old, ugly cabin with peeling bark and garish lighting. Just a small circus held together by security.

He was just gone. And it was absolutely her fault.

As she'd lingered by the doorway, she was jostled onto the trail by the group behind her. They were upset there hadn't been any blood.

Norah cut back through the trail until she found the exit she'd taken four weeks earlier.

She thought about all the time she had spent here tonight trudging through throngs of screaming, laughing kids and costumed staff. It was all for nothing. And she needed to leave. Right now.

As Norah had walked through the hidden exit pathway in the brush, her breath came faster and her fingertips went numb. The numbness quickly traveled up her arms as her vision began to drift. She wondered if she was having a stroke, or maybe a heart attack.

Surely that wasn't possible at sixteen.

It didn't matter.

Norah opens her eyes and takes in her surroundings.

She's sitting on the edge of the Baby Maze, a small arrangement of hay bales that toddlers and small children can navigate when a "family-friendly" version of the Thicket and plaza is open during the day on weekends in late September and early October. There's no one here now, of course.

Norah lets her gaze wander over the empty corn pits. Sand buckets and plastic shovels are strewn across the surface of the dried kernels, their white tips glowing faintly in the darkness. A row of plastic tire swings that have been cut and painted to look like rocking horses sway gently in the wind.

To her left, she sees the entrance to the real corn maze. A dim street light of sorts casts a narrow halo over a stooped older man wearing a beige security uniform.

He's talking to two people.

Norah squints at them for a moment, feeling something twinge in her already volatile stomach. And then, suddenly everything comes into focus.

The boy isn't familiar. He's wearing the standard-issue teenage boy uniform. Hoodie. Jeans. But there's no mistaking the girl. Norah can see the green paint streaked through her hair and across her face. There's fake blood dribbling down the front of her outfit.

It's Taylor Bennett.

Norah leans forward on her knees a little, studying the boy's profile. She thinks he might be one of Aaron's friends. His expression looks pained, even from here. Maybe a little embarrassed.

Without really meaning to, Norah slowly stands and walks through the Baby Maze and along the wall of hay until she is standing within earshot of Taylor, the boy, and the guard.

"And you got separated, how again?" the older man asks, raising his eyebrows knowingly and shuffling between one foot and the other like his heels hurt him.

Taylor makes an irritated noise in her throat and crosses her arms tighter against her coat. They've clearly been at this for a while. Norah notices that up close, Taylor's makeup is smeared all over her face—mostly in the mouth area. "We just *did*. Everyone was doing their own thing, and—"

"Doing their own thing, huh?" The guard chuckles and then sighs, his mouth turning hangdog again. "Honey, we've been over this. What you mean is, they're kissing in the corn somewhere, and they ain't texted you back. They'll come out when they're good and ready."

The boy in the hoodie clears his throat and glances between the guard and Taylor. "We heard, uh, some screams though. She thinks it was her friend." He nods at Taylor.

Although Norah can only see one side of the guard's face, there's no mistaking that he's rolling his eyes. As if on cue, a loud volley of screams rises above the melee in the dark, churning plaza behind them. "I bet you did, honey. I'm telling you though, this happens all the time. You're *supposed* to get lost in the maze. And people are *supposed* to be screaming. You're at a haunted house."

Norah watches, transfixed.

Taylor crosses her arms against her sides, hugging the torn sweatshirt and coat. She glances at the boy, but he shrugs. None of them have noticed Norah yet. "I told you, though. She's not answering her texts. Which isn't like Maren at allfu And the scream sounded . . . different. I *know* it's a haunted house. I'm not stupid."

Norah suddenly remembers a birthday party she went to in middle school, at Taylor's house. Her dad had made the cake. It wasn't anything like the fondant unicorns she'd seen at the other girls' parties. He had tried to use whipped cream for frosting, and the whole thing had melted in the backyard sun. Maren had tried to make a joke about it. Taylor had ignored it. But she'd crossed her arms just like that.

As Norah glances between Taylor's ruined makeup and the guard—who is shaking his head at her again—she feels something shift in her alliance.

It's something about the guard's expression and the boy's painful awkwardness. Or maybe it's the sight of Taylor standing with her head down and arms crossed, insisting that something is wrong.

With nobody believing her.

Norah thinks of her call to Officer Willis earlier and feels her cheeks flush warm. She turns to walk away, back into the dark plaza.

Then spins on her heel instead.

Fuck it.

"What exactly is your job here," Norah asks before she's sure the guard on the hay bale can actually hear her. She gestures at the empty Baby Maze, the corn pit, and the dimly visible tire swings sarcastically. "I must be missing something. Aren't you a security guard? They're asking for your help. And you're just going to sit here?"

The man shuffles his feet to stand and face her, turning his back on the boy, who sidesteps to keep a clear view of whatever is going to happen next. Taylor is staring too, her mouth a tiny O of surprise. Norah draws her own mouth taut in a tight line, waiting for the guard's response.

She should have walked away.

The guard studies her for a moment then scoffs. "Do you know how many times this happens every night? The corn maze is like one big backseat in a Chevy. The only ones who ever go in it, after dark anyway, are the ones who want to get *busy*. And then I hear 'I can't find Jenny,' from their baby sister when she gets cold. Just cool it," he growls. "And stop wasting my time. It's not even haunted. There's a whole lot of corn out there. And then some more corn. The 'missing kids' come out like clockwork after about an hour. If I leave my post for half an hour to go looking for all of them, that's a problem for everyone."

Norah bites down on her cheek before she responds. She's going to tell him who she is. Why she has every right to ask him to do his job, even if it is the goddam corn maze.

But she doesn't. Because even though she can feel the patronizing disdain coming off him, she won't trade it for pity.

"I'm making a complaint when I leave," she states evenly, forcing herself not to break eye contact as she says it. "Come on." She gestures to the dark mouth of the maze, wondering what she is doing even as she nudges Taylor forward in front of her.

"Knock yourselves out," the guard says, waving them on. "Enjoy."

Taylor looks stricken at first, tripping over an ear of corn sticking out of the partially frozen ground. She looks back at the boy, who hesitantly steps past the guard as well.

Norah's heart crashes against her ribcage. And with each step she takes as she walks a little further into the dark maze, the regret hits harder. She's still slightly high. But not nearly high enough for this.

"Uh, thanks so much," Taylor says, still glancing back at the guard as they reach the first fork in the maze. He's leaning back against the stacked hay, shaking his head and smiling.

Norah doesn't reply. Because she doesn't feel like being gracious. And because she's self-aware enough to understand that she's not doing this to be kind or generous or even to help Taylor. She's doing it because she needed to tell someone to go to hell.

Because the anger, at least, is a spark in the darkness.

However, she is now on a wild goose chase to search for the girls who ditched her after middle school—and were just making fun of her dead brother.

As they walk deeper into the dark maze, Norah tries to form a plan of how they will search. "Check down that way," she mutters, motioning for the boy to peer down a narrow, chattering causeway that appears to be a dead-end.

All the paths appear to be dead-ends.

She hears Taylor shuffle a little faster beside her and clear her throat. "I—I just wanted to say sorry. About before."

There is a pause, presumably for Norah to say something about how it's okay. Or about how she's not mad.

When Norah keeps walking, Taylor clears her throat again. "About your brother, too. Brandon. I'm really sorry about that too."

A feeling that's too far away to deal with right now rolls in her chest. So Norah pretends again that she doesn't hear Taylor above the rattle of the stalks.

From within the quiet of the maze, they hear a high-pitched wail float over the shifting corn, and Norah grits her teeth.

She'll look for another fifteen minutes.

And then she's leaving.

CHAPTER 39

Charlie's feet hurt like a son-of-a-gun.

He bought a pair of orthotic shoes from a teenager who looked barely qualified to operate the cash register—let alone help him do battle with the forces making his feet feel like hot pokers. That probably should have been his first clue.

Still, he'd been hopeful. The smiling folks in the photos at the orthopedic shoe shop were walking around pain-free with their grandkids. Plus, there was the thirty-day money-back guarantee.

He looks down at the orthopedic shoes, crusted in a thick layer of mud by this point. He grins, imagining himself handing them back to the perky kid behind the counter for a refund. Thirty days, no questions asked.

Thicket management had found him a place to sit this year, at least. Last year this time, he'd had to ice his feet for twenty minutes at the end of every shift. And even then, he looked like a damn hunchback hobbling around on his nights off.

And yet here he is, standing at his post.

It's been ten minutes since the boy and the girl came out of the maze, saying they couldn't find their friend.

He'd handled the situation okay at first. Particularly when what he'd wanted to say was, "No kidding, kid? You can't find your friend in the *corn maze*?"

But the girl wearing the big sweatpants was something else. She'd looked a little strung out.

Dave would probably chew him out over the whole thing. If the crazy girl who'd come charging out of the Baby Maze actually followed through with her threat, anyway. Still, Dave would understand. He was a decent manager. Not one to hand you your ass over every little thing, especially with the whole circus over the past month.

There had been more crazy than usual running through the Thicket this year, given what had happened—and that was really saying something. When you threw teenagers, sugar, and blood together, you had a legitimate nightmare on your hands under the best of circumstances. Someone was always tearing through something, screaming about something, peeing on something, taking their clothes off, or yelling at him about god-knew-what this time.

The "see something, say something" signs had only made things worse. He'd lost track of the murderers, ghosts, and devil-worshipers someone saw in the corn, or the plaza, or the mini-donut stands. Dave had taken him aside after the first week and told him to take the new security measures with a grain of salt. This was still Declo, Idaho, after all.

Charlie kicks at the hay bale a little, trying to scrape off some of the frozen mud and wondering how many years he even has left at a job like this. Not many. He feels his chest get tighter and stops the line of thought. The jobs he takes throughout the year are crap most of the time. Teenagers are morons, and his body hurts. But at the end of the night, he's still glad to be working at all. Retirement feels like one foot in the grave.

Grumbling, Charlie shuffles out of the orange light above the hay bales, to peer into the maze.

He can't hear the kids calling anymore—but with the wind and the general mayhem floating across the plaza, he wouldn't.

He shakes his head and turns back toward the stacked bales of hay, telling himself that he will rest his feet and enjoy the relative silence of the surrounding kiddie area. Someone else will come screaming out of the maze soon enough. He should sit while he can.

But in the stillness, the expression on the girl's face presses at the back of his mind. He feels a twinge of guilt. She'd seemed like a nice enough kid. Not hysterical. And not dressed like the cast of Cabaret. He remembers seeing her walk in with a group. They've been in the maze a while.

If he had to guess, there are maybe ten people total—including the girl and boy—in the maze right now. Everyone else is waiting in line somewhere for the cabins or the mini donuts. He really isn't busy.

He listens again, and this time he hears a high, short-lived screech. He thinks it's from the maze. But it's not really possible to tell.

Charlie has heard a lot of screams this year. Including, he assumes, the night the kid—and the scarer—were killed. Sometimes he wonders who else heard it happen. If one of the wailing, staccato screams drifting from the trails was one of them.

He'll never know.

Which will never cease to bother him.

Two girls who entered the maze just a few minutes earlier tromp back through the entrance, smiling at him as they pass by and checking their feet for mud. It's the usual protocol.

Most kids step inside the maze, check it out, get some mud on their shoes, and decide they've had enough. The maze is dark and boring and impossible to navigate very well in the dark. The kids who spend the most time in the maze hole up in the furthest corner they can find and paw at somebody else's costume.

There's another loud scream, this one definitely from within the maze itself. The sound pierces the quiet again as the wind cuts out for a moment.

The noise stops abruptly. Like before.

Charlie stands up, wincing as his heels protest with a sensation that's a little like stepping on broken shards of glass.

"Sonofabitch," he mutters, shaking his head and trudging into the darkness of the maze. He'll never understand why they make the damn thing so big every year. Supposes it's for the press. It's a whole campaign every year. "Best Corn Mazes in the US." "Best Haunted Houses in the US." They up the ante a little every time.

He kicks at a full ear of corn lying on the ground in front of him. Some little jerk stuck a row of them tip-down in the mud.

As if there weren't enough hazards in the dark.

After a few minutes, Charlie parts the corn to get to the outer maze. Then he stops, listening. When he's pretty sure he's close to the spot the scream came from, he steps back into the main maze, disoriented for a few seconds until he spins in a slow circle, studying the high walls of corn.

There are really only two main arteries that thread through the maze—and about a hundred dead-ends in between. You can tell the arteries from the dead-ends by the subtle way the corn is bent. Out and back, instead of sideways. The arteries are made with a dozer, not a mini Cat.

He thinks for a moment, propping the ball of one foot against the other to take some of the pressure off his heel.

As he stands still, he hears it: a couple of short snaps, then a flurry of footsteps, coming from the dead-end he just passed.

Charlie turns slowly. Then he hears the low moan. And the laugh.

He rolls his eyes and walks toward the sound.

Bingo.

But before he's even rounded the corner to the dead-end, he slows down.

Somehow, he knows with sudden clarity that he hasn't found the kids.

He can't say why. It's something about the base note in the sound, maybe.

And he's right.

The person standing in the shadows of the dead-end is alone.

At first, Charlie can't quite take in what he's seeing. But yes, the dark figure is wearing a mask.

It's a black, rubber mask with a wide, thick curved beak. The eyeholes are two voids.

The cornstalks behind the man are broken, flattened in some places and leaning at an angle in others.

Charlie puts a hand on the radio at his hip, hoping that when he speaks his voice doesn't break. "Sonofabitch. Stay right there and hand over the mask. *Now.* You can toss it to me. And then you're coming with me. Do you think you're some kind of funny—"

It doesn't register at first, why the words have suddenly stopped coming out of his mouth.

The man in the shadows has darted forward with surprising speed.

At first, Charlie thought the man was trying to run past him into the main artery of the maze.

But no. He sees the arm lift, then fall, then lift again in quick succession.

The pain in his throat hits on a delay.

And when it does, the searing, ripping agony lasts only a moment.

CHAPTER 40

When Taylor hears her phone chime, she scrambles to pull it out of her hoodie pouch.

It will be Maren or Jamie. nonchalant and hinting at how many bases they've just rounded somewhere inside the maze. They'll tell her to meet by the mini-donut stand, or the entrance as soon as posible, because they're hungry again.

Instead, it's her dad.

Hey kiddo. Going to bed soon. Drive safe, go slow.

Taylor bites her lip and buries the phone back inside the pocket of her hoodie, relief curdling into the first inklings of despair.

It's been forty-five minutes since she saw Maren or Jamie. And it's been twenty since they talked to the guard sitting at the entrance. Her voice is getting hoarse. So is Ben's. And her phone is down to twenty percent.

Maren hasn't texted her back. Neither has Jamie. Neither has Aaron or Tyson—or even the freckle-faced kid whose name Taylor can't remember anymore. She wishes, for the millionth time, that they'd never met the boys. That they'd gone to Maisie's stupid party after all. Jamie would be making out with Russ right now—or arguing with him about Angel Girl. Maren would be slipping the vodka into some Hawaiian Punch or leaning over a kitchen counter to make her boobs look bigger, while she flirted with seniors. And Taylor would be tucked into some corner of the living room, fending off comments about the zombie costume. But they would be together. They wouldn't be here.

It's getting colder out. The mud still slips beneath their feet at a few low points on the ground, but everyone's breath is visible now. Small puffs as they walk deeper into the maze.

Norah doesn't call for anyone. She walks ahead, methodically checking every dead-end and artery they come to, while Taylor or Ben wait at the intersections, so no one else gets lost.

Taylor isn't sure why Norah is helping them look. Why she volunteered—especially after what happened earlier. The expression on her face when she walked up to the guard was both terrifying and awe-inspiring.

Taylor tried a little small talk—after she apologized. But any questions she managed to come up with felt either audacious or silly—given the circumstances. How have you been? *Since we stopped talking in middle school.* What have you been up to? *While you've been out of school after your brother's murder.* How are you handling all this? *No, no, and no.*

The path they're walking on veers slightly to the right, and Taylor wonders if they've reached the far edge of the maze. She can't be sure, but it looks like the stalks aren't quite as dense along this wall. Tiny slivers of dusky blue peep through some of the stalks, instead of a dense wall of black.

She can't remember the last time she's ever actually completed a corn maze—let alone this one. But they've got to be approaching the far side. As Norah walks further ahead, Taylor tentatively parts the corn, trying to see through the stalks. She squints, pushing her way into the corn just a little as she tries to get a better idea of their position in the maze.

Taylor lets the stalks fall back in place and steps back, walking faster to catch up with Ben and Norah, who are almost out of sight.

She swallows, trying to soothe her burning throat, before calling out again into the darkness. The wind whisks the sound away almost as soon as the words leave her lips, tangling the stalks in a raspy patter. No matter how loudly she screams, the wind seems to carry her voice down into the stalks, instead of across the maze. She waits for the breeze to die, then tries calling again.

A few steps ahead of her, Ben turns back with a tight-lipped smile and waits, offering his hand when she gets close enough. She could tell by his expression earlier that the confrontation with the guard had embarrassed him a lot. He'd wanted to meet up with Freckle Face—Ryan?—in the plaza, then wait for the others to text.

When Norah had come stomping toward them from the Baby Maze, Ben's jaw had visibly dropped.

All things considered—including the fact Taylor met him two hours ago—Ben has been a pretty good sport. He hasn't come right out and said they should stop combing through the maze, anyway. Maybe she'll give him her number after all when this is over.

Suddenly remembering her dad's text, Taylor lets go of Ben's hand to pull her phone back out of her pocket. The blue light momentarily makes her squint.

She considers telling her dad the truth. That she is at the far end (hopefully) of a dark maze with two virtual strangers, searching in vain to find Maren and Jamie. That she wants him to pick her up. That she needs him to help find her friends. That she is scared.

She starts to type it. Then backspaces. He's already in bed. And he'll only worry. She does her best to spare him that whenever possible. And he does his best to pretend he doesn't worry.

Sweet dreams! Be home in a while! xoxo

Taylor closes the thread and looks at the last group text she sent to Maren and Jamie.

Pls just txt back so I know ur ok?

She scrunches up her nose and reads the text she sent before it.

Srsly where ru guys?

And the text before.

Getting cold. Can we go? Where ru?

She's pretty sure either Maren or Jamie would have texted back if they'd seen any of the messages.

This means either they haven't seen the texts—or there's something wrong.

She shivers, tucking her chin into her sweater and walking faster to catch up with Ben. As she tucks the phone back into her pocket, she feels for the switch on the side—again—to make sure that the ringer is on.

When she reaches Ben, she takes his hand again. If they don't find Maren and Jamie in ten more minutes, they'll head back to the plaza. Find a different guard. Someone who will listen.

She's about to open her mouth to call Maren's name again when she sees that Norah has suddenly stopped walking a few yards ahead.

Ben sees it too. He casts Taylor a helpless glance and shuffles from one foot to the other, trying to stay warm. She can see that he's not even annoyed anymore. Just really, really over this whole night.

Taylor opens her mouth to ask what Norah is doing, hoping it won't come out sounding whiny. Or annoyed.

And that's when she hears it.

The low-pitched moan.

At first, she can't tell why the sound is different from the rest of the distant cacophony.

It's soft enough to be just audible when she is still. When the wind takes a breath.

While she can't be sure, Taylor is somehow positive that the sound is not coming from the direction of the plaza.

And it isn't coming from within the maze, either. She's certain now, from the shape of the maze, that they've hit the back wall.

It sounds like the moaning sound is coming from close by.

Norah takes a step closer to the dark wall of corn and pushes a thick stand of stalks aside. Like Taylor did earlier.

But instead of peering through the stalks, Norah pushes forward, into the opening she's created.

"What are you—" Ben begins.

Norah whirls around. "Shut up," she hisses. Then she parts the corn again, deeper this time, and disappears.

There's rustling. Then a few soggy pops.

Suddenly, Taylor can't see or hear Norah anymore at all. She looks at Ben, who shakes his head as he walks over to the spot where Norah just disappeared. "It's just another trail," he whispers, parting the corn and peering through.

Taylor's chest gets tighter as she imagines walking back through the maze. Again. They should go back for the guard. Call her dad. Or—

"Hold on. Look at this."

She looks up just in time to see Ben disappear through the stalks.

"Come on." His voice sounds excited.

She hurries to catch up with him, parting the scratchy, damp stalks and tensing as the spidery tassels brush against her face when she squeezes through the dense stalks of corn.

On the other side is another narrow trail, flanked by stalks of corn on both sides. This part of the maze is still walled off from the rest of the world, but there don't appear to be any other arteries branching off.

What's more, the wall of corn running along the other side of them isn't a dense partition anymore.

It's more of a blind. Just a few stalks thick. The night beyond filters through in muted shades of navy and a pattern of shadowy silhouettes in the distance.

"I think Norah went through there." Ben points to the thin wall of corn in front of them. He is still whispering.

The moan comes again. Low. Muted. Just a fragment, before it's inaudible.

It sounded so close.

Ben hears it this time too. He takes a step toward the thin wall of corn. "Did you hear that? Is Norah—"

And then, suddenly, a pair of hands—and then Norah herself—pushes back through the corn.

For the first time, she looks unsure. "Is this part of the Thicket?" she whispers, parting the thin blind of corn so they can see through to the other side.

Taylor peers into the darkness, trying to make sense of the shadows.

There's a narrow dirt path on the other side, beyond the maze.

She sees what appear to be the hulking shapes of farming equipment, parked in the weeds. A narrow irrigation ditch. Some sprinklers. The dark shape of a trailer parked on the fringes of yet another field.

There is also the dark outline of a structure, set back from the road along the field.

Taylor's mouth feels dry. She can't hear the moan anymore over the roar of blood in her ears and the chatter of the stalks. "No," she whispers haltingly. "I-I don't think so anyway. Is that where the—"

But Norah is already walking.

So is Ben.

And then, because she doesn't want to be left alone slightly more than she doesn't want to walk into the darkness past the maze, she follows.

CHAPTER 41

This wasn't part of the plan.

The radio on the dead guard's belt sparks to life, spitting static for a few moments until someone's voice breaks through. "Charlie, copy."

The radio is too loud.

He reaches for it, to turn the switch to *off*.

The voice comes again. "What's your twenty?"

He can easily disappear back into the maze and out the front entrance. He doesn't want to. But he's learned when to back away.

While you're ahead.

Part of the guard's throat is flapping open. A dark hole at his sternum.

The blood is already starting to pool and clot in the breeze, a dark, sticky waterfall that will thicken, slow, then stop altogether in the deepening cold.

He sits back on his heels to think.

The body is lying at an angle, in a flattened patch of cornstalks between the inner and the outer maze.

If it were daylight, the struggle—and the subsequent destruction of the corn just a hair's breadth beyond the passageways of the maze—would be impossible to conceal.

That much blood is hard to hide.

But not in the dark.

He rises from his crouched position, feeling the stalks stroke his coat like gentle fingers. He was smart to check the guard post one more time.

But too much time has passed during this detour, and he is bothered by the distance between himself and the dark mill halfway across the maze. He's lost at least twenty minutes, he guesses.

The radio sputters to life again.

"Copy, Charlie."

And again, he reaches to turn the radio off.

But as he touches the rubber buttons, tacky beneath his latex gloves, he suddenly understands that he is still ahead.

He holds the two-way radio for a moment, studying it. The screen is neon green, and the channel is set to twenty-two.

He presses call.

The voice on the other end speaks again. "Hey, Charlie."

The voice is impatient. Distracted. The inflection drops on the last syllable. It's not a question. Just a greeting.

He looks at the guard's face. Eyes half-open, lids heavy with wrinkles and moles. Mouth still set in a drooping line, a partial grimace. He thinks of the man's shuffling steps. Then he clears his throat and speaks. Low and just quiet enough. "Hey. Some kids being rowdy. On my way back out."

The static fills the void again, and the same voice responds right away. "Ok. Just checking in."

He waits a few seconds before he lifts his finger off the call button. Then he slips the radio into his coat pocket next to the still-warm, slightly sticky knife.

He crouches beside the dead man in the dark. The bottom half of his silver badge winks softly in the moonlight. The top half of the badge is obscured by blood.

The text at the bottom reads "Declo Peace Officer."

He smiles and plucks the badge from where it's clipped onto Charlie's breast pocket, then uses the guard's own untucked shirttail to wipe the blood away.

As he stands, he also picks up the wide-brim hat that is lying in the middle of the path a few yards away.

CHAPTER 42

As Norah pushes open the door to the ramshackle building, she can hear the moans without pausing to listen, even with the rustle of Taylor and the boy—Ben, apparently—behind her.

Her fingers feel suddenly clumsy and cold, like they're not really part of her body anymore. The rough surface of the crumbling wood door registers, but barely. Her heart is sucking up all the blood, she thinks, feeling it pound still harder.

When the door swings fully open, the quiet moans stop.

The windowless room is too dark to see much of anything.

As Taylor fumbles for her cell phone's flashlight in the sudden stillness, she can feel some part of herself bracing— and also hoping—for the moment where she shines the light and sees that she is crazy. That this is a prank. That the weed Aaron gave her is making her paranoid. That there is a reasonable explanation for the soft, strangled moans coming from inside this tall, dark building.

As the phone screen's dim blue light cuts the darkness immediately in front of her, the moans start again.

Her throat constricts, and she takes another step into the room.

Taylor and Ben are behind her now, so close they're brushing the back of her hoodie. As the muted sounds take on a new, higher pitch, Taylor shrinks against her.

Norah can't find the flashlight app. She's used it a thousand times. She knows where it is. But she can't think. Not with the sounds in her ears, insisting that she act right now and not a second later.

"Here," Ben rasps from behind her, thrusting his own lit cell phone into her hand.

He doesn't want to be the one to shine the light.

So she does, swinging the beam in front of her, catching dim brown floorboards, sawdust, a bench tipped on its side, and then—

The body, limbs splayed and heavy across the dusty ground, is completely still. It's positioned in such a way that Norah knows it is either fake—or dead.

The girl is slumped face down in the sawdust, both legs kicked out behind her at an angle that makes Norah's stomach hurt.

A thick pool of blood has stained the ground red in a wide, irregular blotch that's been absorbed by the sawdust. The girl's head is at the epicenter of the thick red puddle. Layers of some kind of tape keep her legs bound together up to her waist. One arm hangs limply at her side, a long gash just visible through unraveling strands of dark, wet tape. The other arm is pulled taut behind her back, bound to her legs.

And then Norah notices the corset. It's covered in sawdust, with neon purple ribs.

It's Maren.

Norah wants to swipe the flashlight off. To turn away. To run.

But in the darkness beyond Maren, the mewling, sick-sounding moans have reached a fever pitch.

It takes a moment before Norah realizes, unable to turn away from what looks like Maren's body but can't be Maren's body, that the screams are coming from behind her now, too. Louder, and hardly muffled at all.

It's Taylor.

Norah swings the flashlight to the left as she grabs Taylor's arm, clinging to the numbness in her chest like a life raft. "You have to stop," she chokes. "Taylor, you have to stop right now."

Taylor clamps her mouth shut, turning the scream into a soft, keening moan that matches the others.

"Oh my god," Ben is repeating in a quiet monotone. He suddenly grabs the phone flashlight out of her hand, shining it to the far left again.

When Norah follows the beam, she sees the source of the moans.

There are two more boys and a girl, staggered along the wall on their sides, facing her.

Jamie. Tyson. Aaron. And the freckle-faced kid.

Like Maren, their arms and legs have been bound tightly together with tape, then tied behind them. As the light shines on them, they thrash harder in the sawdust, their movements desperate, but only in inches, as their legs stay fixed together like grotesque mermaid tails while their hands remain pinned behind their backs.

A thick layer of black tape has been wrapped around each of their heads just below the nostrils. The tape has been wrapped around Jamie's long auburn hair at the nape of her neck. Strands of hair stick out in sections at unnatural angles. She looks like a disheveled doll in a drawer.

"Call the police. Right now," Norah rasps, trying to hold Ben's phone's flashlight steady while she reaches back inside her pocket for her own cell phone.

Five percent battery. Norah swings the flashlight around to Taylor, who has started to shake, her eyes fixed on Maren's black and purple corset. "Taylor. Taylor, please. Do you have your phone? Mine's almost dead."

Dead.

The word comes out before she can stop it, and even though it is just a word, the room seems to shrink around it. She can smell the blood, now that she knows what it is. The moans fade as her vision begins to swim, the silence deafening in her ears. She can see the dots dancing across her field of vision again, can feel the nausea rising again.

Norah blinks, forcing herself to take a breath. Whoever did this isn't likely to be gone for very long.

"Taylor," she says again, swinging the flashlight back toward Jamie, Aaron, Tyson, and Freckle Face along the wall, then down at Taylor's feet—away from Maren's body on the ground. "Taylor, look at me. Do you have your phone?"

Taylor gasps and nods, fumbling in her sweatshirt pocket then holding the metallic phone in front of her like an offering in the dim beam of light.

"Good. Go outside and call 9-1-1. Me and Ben—" she gestures into the darkness with the flashlight, shining it on Ben, "we're going to untie them. Do it now, Taylor. Hurry."

To her relief, Taylor stumbles backward, the lit screen of her phone dimly lighting her way. Norah watches to see that she has the phone to her ear as she hovers in the doorway. Then she turns toward Ben, who is still standing behind her.

He's breathing so hard she can feel the puffs of air break against her cheek as she grabs his wrist. "I'm going to put your phone light on the floor—there—so we can see," she says as she crouches to prop the phone up against a wooden bench. It casts a thin beam of light in the direction of Jamie and the boys, who have stopped struggling so much. They are squinting expectantly, desperately in the dim light. "Now hurry, help me untie them."

Just do the next thing, Norah tells herself as she kneels in the sawdust beside Jamie with her long auburn hair. She hesitates for a moment, looking at Jamie's unblinking eyes and flared nostrils, beads of sweat reflected in the beam of the flashlight. The whites of her eyes are tinged red, and Norah forces herself to look back at the tape. She needs to untie the legs first.

So they can run.

Norah is dimly aware of what Taylor is saying as she stammers into the phone just outside the doorway. She keeps her hand cupped around her ear and holds the phone close, to hide any light.

Norah can't hear everything, but just knowing that Taylor has the police on the line is enough to bring the blood slowly filtering back to her numb fingers. She works faster, less clumsily, as she unwinds yet another layer of tape from Jamie's legs.

With each layer she peels off, Jamie tenses as if this time she'll finally feel the last strip of tape burn the bare skin of her legs.

Beside her, Ben is feverishly pulling at the tape on Aaron's legs.

It's difficult to see as their shadows bob in the bare light. But finally—finally—Norah sees pale skin as she rips at the last strip of black tape on one leg.

But as she unwinds the last strip, wincing at the angry red welts that pop up on Jamie's skin, she sees that Jamie's feet are bound with some kind of thin rope, too.

Just do the next thing, Norah thinks again, scanning around wildly, willing her mind to think of a way to cut the rope.

Suddenly, Taylor is standing above her.

"They're coming, Jamie," she says in a choked whisper, sliding her cell back into her pocket.

Norah tenses. "Why did you hang up? Stay on the phone with the police—call them back," she says more harshly than she'd intended.

Taylor lets out a sound that is half hiccup, half moan. "I'm on 4G, it's eating my battery up. They—they asked how much battery I had left. They told me to put it in low power mode in case we needed to call them back again. I'm down to 10 percent."

She kneels down beside Norah. "They're coming, Jamie," she repeats. Jamie has begun to cry. "Norah almost has you. I'm going to help the boys," Taylor says, sliding between Tyson and the freckle-faced boy on the floor. Then she hurries to pull the first strip of duct tape on Tyson's legs.

Jamie shakes her head, her tear-streaked eyes bloodshot and wild, muffled screams falling mute against the duct tape that has been wound at least a dozen times around her jaw and hair.

Norah closes her eyes, her fingers still clawing at the thin, dense rope that is so tight it's cutting into the skin on Jamie's legs. *Think. Think now.* She scans the dark room, looking for something she can use to cut, or at least fray, the rope.

Behind her, in the shadows, she sees the edge of the wooden bench. "Hang on," she whispers to Jamie, rising to her feet and grabbing the phone that is propped against the bench. "I need to find—"

She sees what she's looking for: a long, thick nail poking halfway out of one of the bench legs that wobbles. She can hear Ben and Taylor still ripping at the duct tape in the dark, fumbling and frantic.

She pulls on the nail.

It doesn't budge.

She pulls harder, digging her fingers into the nailhead and leaning backward as she braces her feet against the other bench legs. After a few seconds, she feels it come loose in her hand with a rusty scritch.

The bench topples to the left, landing with a soft thud.

On top of Maren.

Norah's stomach lurches, and she fights the urge to right the bench. To stroke Maren's hair. To remove her tape and ties too.

They'll untie her when they get here, she tells herself as she swallows a painful lump in her throat, willing the dispatcher to hurry, praying that Taylor knew what to say.

Fingers throbbing, Norah props the phone flashlight back up against the toppled bench, feeling for the long nail's sharp point. Will it work? It has to. How soon until the police arrive? Will it be soon enough? Should they all be here, inside like this? Should she send Taylor—or Ben—back through the maze? Is it safer inside or out? Are they better off together? How is she somehow in charge here? How long would it take for all of them to run back through the maze? What about the road?

She feels herself start to shut down, to float away in the haze. *Just the next thing,* she tells herself again, taking the nail in one hand and digging it into the thin rope. She jiggles the sharp end around as fast as she can, trying—and failing—to stay away from the skin on Jamie's legs.

The rope is so thin, dense, and tight that it's all but impossible. Jamie starts to cry harder, and red spots of blood appear as the nail misses the thin target of the rope. It's hard to tell if Norah is making any progress at all. "I'm so sorry Jamie, just a little more," she chokes out, feeling for the knots in the rope instead.

"I'm down to the rope too," Ben whispers next to her, and she feels his hand tap her shoulder.

Norah keeps her eyes on the yellow rope. Strand by strand. Knot by knot. It has to give way at some point if she keeps going. "The bench," she whispers, "a few feet to your left." She brushes the coils of ripped-off black tape away from Jamie's legs, so she can see better. The rope is attached to her other foot, too.

Behind her, Norah hears the low thud of the bench leg wobble on the ground. Then the sound of another nail ripping into the rope as Ben digs. She hears Taylor, who is still working at the duct tape, whispering assurances to the freckle-faced boy.

Norah manages to get through a second knot. She's maybe halfway through one section of rope. Just *one*. She listens with one ear for the sound of sirens, the sound of a police intercom. Every few seconds, she glances back at the dark rectangle of doorway looming behind her that might slowly open any second.

How much time has gone by? Has it been a minute since Taylor made the call? Five minutes? Twenty?

Norah suddenly pictures the man she saw slipping inside the canvas tent and feels a wave of nausea as she tries to bring his face into focus.

Was it him?

Her thoughts feel both runny and sharp. And hovering on the fuzzy edges is the knowledge that whoever did this is probably the same person who killed Brandon.

Norah pushes the thought back to the periphery. There's no space for it right now. She quickly scoots to her right through the sawdust, feeling for the toppled bench to extract another nail for Taylor.

Just the next thing.

Norah finds another nail and pulls, ignoring the sound of the bench as it hits a soft landing again. She no longer feels the sting of the metal as it digs into her index finger and thumb.

Jamie has stopped struggling. The thin, barely audible keening sounds still come from her taped mouth have stopped too. She's lying with her face in the sawdust now, her auburn hair draped and dusty around her. Norah knows she is alive because of the rise and fall of her back as she leans into the ropes. But that's it.

Norah glances back at the doorway again, swiping at a sweaty lock of bangs that has fallen into her eyes.

The police are on their way, she reminds herself, adding to her mantra as she feels another knot strain and give. *They're on their way.*

CHAPTER 43

When he reaches the edge of the fields beyond the outer maze, he stops.

The door to the mill is open, a narrow black rectangle silhouetted against the murky fields behind it.

As he cautiously approaches the side of the mill, he can hear them. There is quick shuffling. Then the faint scratch of the tape being removed.

He listens, waiting for more information.

As if in response, the radio screen blinks to light, a soft green, as the quiet static indicates a new call coming in.

Taking a few steps back into the hardscrabble fields, he slowly turns up the volume, holding the speaker cupped close.

"Charlie? Copy, now. We have a call in from Rupert PD dispatch . . ."

The voice trails off into static, and he closes his eyes, tasting the flavor of the voice.

Urgent. But asking for reassurance.

The static increases in volume. "A girl called. Says there's people hurt, maybe dead, in the old mill outside the maze where the gallows used to be."

He lets his finger trace the red CALL button, making room for the possibilities to expand, feeling the balance of control tilt up and down, like a weighted scale.

When the scales settle, he presses the CALL button. He knows his own voice will be as static and mechanical as the one on the other end.

"We've got a situation here, all right," he says. "I've got a twenty on the mill now," he adds, pleased by the gruffness and annoyance in his low voice. "Teenagers got into the staff tent and took some props, fake blood. Scared a couple of kids in the maze half to death, though it was pretty funny."

Just enough detail. Not too much. He lets the static burble through the air for just a moment, then continues. "You still on with PD? I've got it all covered."

He leaves it at that. Then waits. The scales tip up and down, up and down, as the seconds draw out.

The possibilities are slipping, tilting.

The screen blinks green.

More static.

"Thank god. Yeah, we're still on the line. I'll let them know. Thanks, Charlie"

He presses the CALL button one more time. "I'll bring 'em up front, and you can decide how you want to deal with this. Give me fifteen."

"Ok, Charlie."

Charlie. He smiles wider, tasting the relief in the man's voice on the other end of the radio.

The radio screen goes black and stays black.

He closes his eyes one more time, still weighing the scales, feeling them tip back in his favor.

Keeping the radio held aloft in one hand, he walks back toward the mill, not bothering to hide his crunching footfalls anymore.

He only has about fifteen minutes, give or take, before someone begins to wonder why no one has re-emerged from the corn maze.

But fifteen minutes will be plenty of time.

He pauses at the edge of the dark mill, then pulls the sweaty beard over the top of his head and stuffs it into the pocket of his coat next to the mask.

It won't matter if they see his face now.

CHAPTER 44

"Police!"

The word feels like a light switch. Suddenly Norah's fingers, which have been mechanically, frantically, and somehow still gently ripping at the knots in the unforgiving rope begin to tremble violently as the relief floods her system.

To her left, she hears a muffled double-plink as Taylor and Ben drop their nails into the sawdust, scurrying to their feet.

"We're here," Taylor croaks, clearing her throat quickly and then trying again. "We're in here!"

The heavy footsteps stop, and the green light from a radio appears in the doorway.

Norah shoves her hands into her pockets, feeling the tremors travel up and down her arms and legs. She's never felt relief like this. She swallows the thick lump that has suddenly risen in her throat.

She's not sure how long it would have taken them to get through all the rope, all the knots. The only way was to fray them, strand by strand.

It was taking too long. How long, she can't say. It feels like mere minutes have passed, but surely it was longer.

It doesn't matter. *This is the end,* she tells herself, biting down on her lip to keep it from shaking too. Everything is going to be okay. She saved them. She did what she couldn't do for Brandon.

Norah tries again to remember how long it has been since Taylor called the police. It feels like it's been only minutes. But Norah is all too familiar with how time can distort.

At her feet, Jamie is suddenly thrashing again, wailing through her taped mouth. Norah feels a pang of guilt that Jamie is still in the same position she found her. Bound, mouth taped, gagged.

But help—*real* help—is here.

"Shh, he'll be able to get the ropes off, Jamie," Norah soothes, shoving her shaking hands into her hoodie pockets and trying to calm down.

To her right, at the edge of the phone's flashlight beam, the boys are straining at their ropes too, whipping their heads back as far as the tape will allow, to look at the man crossing the threshold at the doorway.

Norah waits for the officer's flashlight beam—a real flashlight—to cut through the darkness. But even the small green square on the radio suddenly goes dark. She can just make out the officer's silhouette as he takes a few steps closer.

"I need all of you against the wall, quick as you can. The other officers are fanning out. We think whoever did this is still close by."

As Norah stumbles to her feet, the familiar buzzing fills her ears, and she hopes that she is not about to pass out. *It's over,* she tells herself again.

She watches as Taylor scoots against the wall, reaching out with one hand to gently stroke Jamie's auburn hair. With the way Jamie is positioned, Taylor can just touch her feet.

Jamie is still thrashing. So are Aaron and the other boy.

Something is wrong.

Norah feels it deep in her gut even as she tries to tell herself that everything is going to be okay now.

Jamie kicks at Taylor's hand, hard enough that Taylor draws her fingers back, glancing at Norah in confusion.

Norah looks at the officer, who is holding one hand aloft, gesturing for Norah and Ben to move toward the wall.

He hasn't said a word about the three people who are hogtied on the floor.

"It's okay. It's okay now," Norah chokes out in a whisper as she moves toward the wall. Again, she has the thought that the officer has arrived very quickly. Too quickly. She can't be sure, but if she had to guess it's only been maybe five minutes since Taylor called the police.

Ben follows Taylor toward the wall.

So does the officer.

Norah squints through the floating flecks of static, scrutinizing the officer's shadowy features that are just visible in the light of the phone flashlight still propped up beside the bench. He's clean-shaven, and his narrow jaw extends above a protruding Adam's apple. His thin lips are set in a straight line.

As the officer takes another step forward, Norah bites the inside of her cheek. His foot is only a few inches away from Maren's exposed thigh.

He doesn't seem to notice.

Norah feels her stomach tighten. "It's okay," she whispers again, as much to herself as the boys and Jamie, whose terrified expressions thrash in and out of the phone's flashlight beam.

"Hang tight with me," the officer is saying. "As soon as we've secured the area, I'll have plenty of backup to . . ."

She misses what he says next.

Because it's then that she sees—really *sees*—his leg. It's still a few inches away from Maren's body on the floor. She can't help but look, unable to bear the thought that he will stumble across Maren like the inanimate bench.

There's something, in the recesses of her memory, that tells her to look twice.

She sees it with a sudden burst of clarity.

The army fatigues.

She stares and turns the image over in her mind. Police uniforms probably vary. The officers she's met—and there have been a lot now—sometimes wore jeans. Khaki pants, usually. Blue slacks.

She's never seen anyone wearing army fatigues.

She thinks of the guard at the entrance and the security guard who was collecting contraband at the metal detector.

Khaki. Blue.

Her stomach coils tighter. *Something is wrong.*

It's only a pair of pants.

It might not mean anything.

And yet.

The green screen of the radio crackles quietly to life. The volume is turned down, but the words still come through.

"Charlie? Can you copy? Rupert PD is headed this way. Management wants to press charges . . ."

Norah's mind spins as she tries to make sense of it. She's suddenly not sure anymore whether the six of them are tucked safely into a corner.

Or just cornered.

The dull roar in her ears gets louder, and the feeling that she is floating just above her center of gravity intensifies.

She has stopped moving.

The officer notices too. He takes a step toward her.

CHAPTER 45

Taylor keeps her eyes on Norah.

Because looking anywhere else is not an option. She can't look at the blur of Jamie's dull copper hair that is tangled with sawdust and matted with tears and dried blood. She can't look at the two boys lying on the floor, screaming through their gags. She can't look at Ryan, the boy with the freckles, huddled beside her and trying to muffle the fact that he is crying.

And she can't look at the officer in the shadows who is standing directly above the dark silhouette of the body that can't be—but must be—Maren.

She feels for the cell phone in her pocket and squeezes it. She should have texted her dad earlier. He would be on his way now.

Her throat constricts. She'd even be happy to see Wendy right now.

Jamie isn't screaming anymore. She's making that barely audible, droning wail from behind the duct tape.

Every few seconds, Taylor tries to stroke her leg. And every few seconds, Jamie coils back and then kicks Taylor's outstretched fingers as hard as she can.

Is she angry that Taylor couldn't get the ropes off faster? Is she out of her mind?

Blinking back tears, Taylor fixes her gaze on Norah. Norah, who has suddenly stopped walking a few feet shy of the wall.

The officer takes a step closer.

"Miss? I'm sorry, but time really is of the essence—"

Norah stays frozen where she is. She's staring at a spot on the ground near the officer's feet. When she looks up, her gaze is directed back at Taylor.

In a voice that is just audible above the scraping sawdust and the muffled, moaning cries, she hisses, *"Run."*

Taylor feels her stomach clench with confusion.

The words don't make sense.

"Taylor, RUN."

This time, Norah screams the words. It's a ragged, loud, *do-it-now* sound.

Taylor's gaze slides to Jamie's tear-streaked face.

Jamie is whipping her head up and down in a frenetic amen.

Yes.

So she does it.

She runs.

CHAPTER 46

Batshit crazy.

The words thunder through Norah's head, louder than her screams.

She doesn't know if she's making the right choice. But she won't risk it. Not again. So she screams anyway, watching with equal parts relief and horror as first Taylor then Ben scrambles to their feet in the shadows.

You are batshit crazy.

The two hesitate for only a moment. And then they tear toward the open mill door, just a few feet away from where the man in the army fatigues is standing. He is holding out his hands palm-up in a gesture that says, *Don't you know I'm here to help you? Please, let me help you.*

Norah follows Taylor and Ben's flight in a syrupy daze, the scream falling silent on her lips.

She watches in what feels like stop-motion as the man in the shadows pulls his hands to his sides.

He tenses.

Then he pivots ever so slightly and lunges toward them in the darkness.

As he steps forward, he places his foot directly on—instead of over—Maren's back with a sickening, muffled pop.

It's just enough force to nudge the wooden bench that is wedged against her thigh.

And that movement is enough force to disturb the phone flashlight that is still propped against the wooden bench as it rocks against the hard ground.

The phone wobbles and falls, leaving the barest sliver of light in the thick, dusty air as Taylor and Ben—and the thin-faced man wearing army fatigues—disappear from view.

Through the blood pounding hard in her ears, Norah hears the discordant thump of footsteps scrambling in the darkness.

Jamie, Tyson, Aaron and the freckle-faced boy—their mouths shut with layers of tape—are still screaming.

And now Norah knows why.

She stumbles to her feet in the darkness, skirting the bench—or where she thinks the bench is—from the position of the dim rectangle of light face-down in the dust. She is sure that at any moment she will collide with the man in the army fatigues.

She stops when she hears a louder scream from just in front of her.

It's not the muffled drone of the mouths that are covered with tape.

It's Taylor's.

There's a second scream.

Ben's.

His scream is punctuated by a series of dull thuds, then cut short with a wet-sounding crack.

Partial scalping.

Massive blood loss due to laceration of the C1 vertebrae.

Aggravated by asphyxia.

Norah can't feel her hands or her legs beneath her. And she's not sure whether the heavy, jagged breathing she can hear above the slick thuds and Taylor's screams is her own, or his.

Until she hears the calm, lilting voice.

He's not even out of breath much. Just calm. Quiet. Authoritative.

"If you run, I'll kill her too. Along with the others, of course."

Too. Kill her *too.*

He pauses. There is more shuffling. And then there is a thick, heavy thud that can only be a body hitting the ground. The sound elicits another short, frantic scream from Taylor.

She's still alive, Norah thinks.

The man's voice cuts through the darkness again. Soft. Calm.

Between the thick, pulsing buzz in her ears and the lead weight of her limbs, Norah can't tell whether the voice is coming from ten feet away or right in front of her.

"Pick up the phone and walk toward me," the voice says softly. "I won't ask twice."

CHAPTER 47

He is holding Taylor by her hair, his fingers clenched through the braid at the nape of her neck.

His grip is so tight that her chin is forced downward, against her neck, and her back leg is pressed against his thigh.

The knife he is holding against the side of her neck, the blade reflecting silky red in the dim light, is sending dark trickles of blood into the collar of her gray sweatshirt.

It takes Norah a moment to register the fact that Taylor is covered in blood. Not the dabs and flecks she painted on as part of her costume. But black-looking sprays and splotches. One arm of her sweatshirt is completely drenched in the dark liquid.

Taylor's chest rises and falls as she tries to hold her balance. Her breath is escaping in fast gasps through her clenched teeth as she struggles to stay close enough that he doesn't press the knife any deeper into her neck.

She stands with one foot behind her, one foot in front, her back arched as she straddles a dark shape lying motionless on the floor at her feet.

Norah feels the bile surge up at the back of her throat.

Ben. He's dead.

Dead. Like her brother. Like Maren, in her Halloween costume a few feet away on the dirty floor.

Dead.

Norah keeps her eyes on Taylor while she strains her ears, listening for any indication that help—real help—is nearby.

All she hears is distant screaming.

Norah doesn't realize she has moved her feet toward Taylor—toward him—until he speaks. "That's a good girl. A few steps closer, please. And hand me the phone."

As he says it, Norah shines the flashlight beam away from Taylor, to his face.

He doesn't blink.

Dots swim in front of her eyes. When she blinks, red and orange afterimages appear in the narrow beam of the flashlight, dancing to the roaring sound in her ears.

How many times has she wondered what she would do if she were to come face to face with the man who killed Brandon? How many times has she thought about what she would have done in the cabin that night if she had stayed with her brother—where she was supposed to be.

And now inexplicably, horrifyingly, here he is—in front of her. A few feet away.

And she is walking, meekly, toward him.

And she is holding a phone. She is holding a phone, for god's sake.

Could she call for help or press the emergency dial in the amount of time it would take him to cross the room—or press the knife into Taylor's neck?

She knows that the answer is no.

Help will not arrive in time.

Norah flicks her gaze down at the man's radio. The screen is black now, but it's still sticking out of his coat breast pocket.

"Walk faster, please. Or I'll have to kill her right now."

She takes another step forward, knowing in her bones that he will do it anyway, no matter what she does.

No matter what Brandon did.

He is only waiting until she hands him the phone.

And then he'll kill her. Then Taylor. Then the others. Just like he killed Brandon.

Somewhere beyond what she can control, she can feel her brain flipping frantically through the possibilities, the escape routes, the Hail Marys in rapid succession. Trying to find a way out. Trying to survive. Trying to change the ending.

She finds nothing.

This *is* the end.

Again.

Even in the shadows, she can see hope burning in Taylor's expression, desperate to believe that it will somehow be okay. That if Norah hands over the phone he'll let them walk free into the maze. That he will disappear back into the dark, murky fields he came from.

But it will not be okay. That's not how it works.

Another step. Two more, and she will be close enough to hand him the phone.

I'm sorry, she thinks. For Brandon. For Taylor. For Jamie with her auburn hair. For everyone who will die in the next few minutes. For her mom and dad, who are probably asleep on the couch by now with half-eaten bowls of cereal in front of them.

Unexpected tears prick at the corners of her eyes as she holds the phone in front of her, extending her hand so she won't have to move any closer. She knows that she is delaying the inevitable for a few seconds at most. But she's unable to stop herself from doing it anyway.

And then, with such abrupt force that it nearly makes her gasp out loud, Norah's brain delivers the Hail Mary—for some of the people in this room, at least.

Norah lowers her eyes and lets her shoulders droop in defeat.

Then she takes another half step forward.

CHAPTER 48

He's almost disappointed to see her give up so easily.

Her bare face is crumpled and wet with tears. Her dirty sweatpants and hoodie are covered in a snowstorm of sawdust. She looks pathetic.

He'd like to play with her hope longer. But he'd also like to move things along.

He decides he'll kill the girl with the braid first, as soon as Sweatpants hands him the phone.

CHAPTER 49

Norah flicks her wrist, and the phone flies through the air toward him, a thin arc of white light.

The darkness swallows Norah whole again. And as it does, as he pulls just slightly away from Taylor, reaching for the phone that will land beyond his reach if he does not.

As he does, Norah's hand darts inside her coat pocket.

It's still there.

The nail.

As her fingers close tight around the long, thin piece of metal she lunges forward, summoning everything awful that has fallen into the black hole inside her chest to the surface.

The rage. The crazy. The horror. The guilt. The batshit.

As she makes contact with the sleeve of his coat in the darkness, she calculates his position and drives her knee against his groin.

He lets out a sharp grunt, and Norah pivots to the side, hoping he will expect to find her in front of him in the dark.

Then she wheels toward him, her feet sliding in the old sawdust.

The unfeelable emotions that have been coursing beneath her skin for the past six weeks rise.

And she lets them out.

This will be the end for her. She knows that. Like it was the end for Brandon.

But maybe it won't be the end for Taylor. Or Jamie. Or the boy with the freckles.

Bracing for the knife in her skin—or Taylor's—Norah forces her field of vision to stay on the dim white patch of skin that she can see just below his bare chin.

Then she drives the nail toward it as hard and as deep as she can.

Just the next thing. Then the next. She watches for the dim flash of white at his collarbone and strikes again and again, even as he stumbles backward against the wall, pulling her with him as she claws at the skin beneath his jacket.

She can feel his hands rough against her throat, grabbing at her hoodie, scrambling for control. And she can hear a tearing sound that is either flesh or fabric as she drives the nail into him again and again.

As they stumble backward a second time, he manages to hook one leg around hers.

Norah falls.

She screams as his full weight crashes on top of her. For a moment, she can't breathe. She can't even move as she feels him pull himself up onto his elbows.

Rivulets of warm liquid spill onto her cheek, and she sucks in a painful breath, waiting to feel his knife slice through her throat. The kinetic rage curdles in her stomach as she lies motionless, the nail still clutched tightly in her right hand.

Norah braces, hoping but not expecting that maybe she will see her brother's face when she opens her eyes again. She tells herself that Taylor is out the door and halfway across the cornfield by now, her phone to her ear.

Instead, Norah feels the heavy weight of the man in the army fatigues suddenly lift.

She squeezes her eyes shut, imagining him lifting the knife in the dark. She wonders where it will land.

But then she hears the heavy, dragging footsteps moving along the wall, heading away from her. His breath is ragged, no longer measured.

He's heading toward the door.

Norah isn't sure whether he's trying to escape, or going after Taylor.

Either way, he should have killed her first.

Rolling onto her side, Norah heaves herself upright and launches toward him in the same motion.

She collides with him against the wall just before he reaches the door, flailing in the darkness for somewhere to strike. Once again, she hones in on the pale, mottled skin bobbing above his coat collar in the dark.

He screams, turning to reach for her as she claws and stabs. Norah uses her hip to barrel into him again, hearing a sound that is equal parts pain and indignation. The noise cuts off abruptly as he falls.

She can feel some part of herself watching in disbelief. But it doesn't slow her down.

There is more blood than she imagined the thin nail could draw. She can no longer see flashes of white skin at his collar. Just darkness.

She pulls the nail back and drives it down, again and again, not sure anymore who is screaming or who is bleeding.

She keeps going until the flurry of her own arm is the only movement she can feel. And until the blood is so slick on her hands that she nearly drops the nail

She keeps going until she suddenly realizes that the knife hasn't entered her throat after all.

Instead, she is on top of him, and his fingers have gone limp at her clothes and her throat.

She realizes with a mix of horror and relief that not only will she survive, but she has actually killed the bastard.

It's only when she hears quiet sobs behind her that she turns around, the backdraft of rage and adrenaline already evaporating.

Taylor.

Norah's hands start to shake again as she pushes away from the lifeless form on the floor, her foot brushing against something solid in the sawdust as she takes a few steps back the way she came.

His knife.

Recoiling, Norah reaches for Ben's cell phone lying face down a few yards to her right, the flashlight app still forming a dim halo in the sawdust.

She casts the beam high into the center of the room, away from the man's body. She's not ready to see him—or what she has done to him—in the light.

Taylor is standing directly in front of her. Her eyes are wide, and her throat is bleeding in a steady dark path down the front of her neck, mixing with the tears that are running down her cheek. She's clutching what's left of her braid with both hands, as if he might suddenly reach for it again.

Norah feels the tears prick at her eyes as she moves forward to hug her, still gripping the nail in one hand and the cell phone in the other. "It's okay. We're okay. Run for help."

As she says it, a green square lights up along the wall with a quiet beeping sound.

His radio.

It's still clipped onto the man's front coat pocket. It crackles to life, with barely audible static.

"Go," she tells Taylor again, louder. "I'll stay with them." She nods into the darkness behind them. "Follow the dirt road outside and stay along the field until you find somebody. Bring them back to help. Do you still have your phone?"

When Taylor nods mutely, Norah reaches into her pocket. She tucks the bloody nail against the fleece of her hoodie and reaches for her own phone. "Look, me too. We'll both call, okay?"

Taylor presses the sleeve of her sweater against her throat. Then she pulls her phone from her front pocket and, before Norah can stop her, she turns the light toward the body a few yards away against the wall.

The man is covered in blood, down to his army fatigues. His eyes are closed. His mouth hangs open in a frozen grimace.

Against his jacket, the radio screen is still bright green. And it's still buzzing with that just-audible static.

Taylor backs away in horror, hesitating at the open doorway. "Okay," she chokes in a hoarse whisper, blinking back tears. Then she takes off in a shaky run, throwing the door open wide with a bang. Her footsteps hit the dirt with soft, grainy thuds then disappear in the rustle of the stalks outside.

Jamie and the boys have stopped thrashing.

They're quiet now.

But in the silence, Norah can still hear the endless screams from the Thicket drifting in fitful whispers over the maze.

CHAPTER 50

Taylor is sure that she has dialed 9-1-1, and she is sure that the call has connected.

But beyond that, all she knows is that she is talking in gasps and spurts as she runs toward the glimmers of light in the distance, keeping the wet, dirty sleeve of her sweatshirt pressed tight against the sticky warmth that is still running in a warm river down her neck.

Her eyes dart in frantic zigzags as runs along the narrow dirt road that flanks the maze.

Between the pounding in her ears and the wind through the stalks, she can barely hear the police dispatcher. Still, she pushes herself faster, willing the burning in her lungs to take precedence over the images of Ben's lifeless body, the blood-soaked sawdust, and the feeling of his hands—and knife—against her neck.

She knows she should slow down to talk to the dispatcher in full sentences to make sure she has been understood, but that would mean stopping.

And she can't do that. Not while Jamie and Norah—and Maren—and the two boys are still in the darkness behind her. Not while *he* is still in the darkness behind her.

"There's a bunch—of old—junk—a trailer—and some—farm stuff—outside it—" she gasps, unable to remember what she's already said or how many times she's already said it. It doesn't matter. She'll keep repeating everything she knows until help arrives. Or until she reaches the plaza.

She pulls the phone away from her ear to look at the battery. One percent.

As she runs, keeping the phone bouncing between her ear and her shoulder, she can hear the woman on the other end of the line in bits and pieces. The calm voice is urging her to slow down, to rack her brain for any more information. The woman says something about security at the Thicket. Something about a prank.

Taylor does stop then, pressing the phone against her ear. A hard shiver runs through her as the dark wall of corn to her left whips in a gust of wind. "I can't hear you very well, Did you say 'prank'? This isn't a prank. There's a man in the shack —" Her voice breaks and she can feel the hysteria rising. "He's dead—but he had a radio. He told us he was a cop."

The woman responds without missing a beat. "Stay with me, Taylor. Officers are almost there. You should see them from the parking lot any time now. Just stay on the phone with me, okay, and keep moving. Can you tell me about the building one more time?"

It's then that Taylor finally sees the faint on-and-off blinking of red and blue in the distance ahead of her. The dark, yawning parking lot can't be more than a few hundred yards away.

"I think I see them," she chokes out, letting the sweatshirt sleeve fall from her throat and pressing the phone hard to her ear as she starts to run again. She tries to focus on what the woman on the phone is saying next, but it's nearly impossible to hear.

Veering away from the narrow dirt path, she crashes through a thin scrub of brush, feeling the branches catch threads of her sweatshirt as she runs. The brush gives way to more fields, the stalks half-broken, the ground torn up.

Finally, she reaches the edge of the lot. When she does, Taylor realizes that she can no longer hear the dispatcher in her ear. The phone is dead.

Shoving the phone into her pocket, she keeps her eyes on the blinking lights and forces herself to move faster, despite the pounding in her head and the taste of blood in her mouth. She doesn't stop until she is standing on the edge of the parking lot.

There are three police cars. One officer is standing beside a brightly lit parked police car, holding a radio. Three others are just visible across the lot, fanning out behind two men in tan uniforms. All of them are heading toward the plaza entrance, toward the other end of the maze.

They're quickly moving away from her.

Stumbling forward, Taylor screams, as loud and as long as she can.

At first, she is sure that the noise has been lost in the melee that is still coming from the plaza.

Then the officer standing by the vehicle turns toward her.

She moves faster, stumbling through the grass, knowing she's nearly invisible in the darkness.

When she veers into the first row of cars, where he can finally see her, she watches him take in her appearance. The blood. The braid undone. The gray and green makeup that must be smeared down her face.

His expression is wary. She realizes that he is probably wondering which parts of her are fake.

She screams again, and the officer moves forward, striding toward her while he holds his radio to his mouth.

When he reaches her, she repeats what she told the dispatcher, feeling the words tumble out of her mouth like vomit, unsure what she's repeating or what makes sense.

She talks around the ache in her throat until she is sure all of the important information is out.

A few minutes later, a woman who arrives with a wailing ambulance places a blanket around her shoulders and guides her out of view of the growing crowd of onlookers. They are gathered around the police lights like moths.

The woman gently helps her onto a white gurney inside the van. There are two other beds beside her, both empty.

The strobing lights and pounding music inside the plaza have stopped. Somewhere beyond the ambulance, someone is talking on a bullhorn, directing everyone out into the dark parking lot and asking them to keep moving.

"What's the best way for us to reach your mom and dad?" the woman is asking. "If you can stick with me just a little longer, I have a few more questions for you. But we want to make sure someone is—"

"My dad," she whispers, realizing that she is holding her dead phone clutched in both hands in front of her. "Did you find them yet?" she asks, telling her fingers to let go of the phone and feeling a sudden violent shudder pass through her.

Maren is dead. Ben is dead.

Her hands are shaking harder now, and she drops the phone on the floor of the ambulance before the woman can take it from her.

His knife, his hands were on her neck less than fifteen minutes ago.

Norah stopped him.

Taylor looks down at her sweatshirt for the first time, realizing how much blood is there. There's no way to tell how much of it is actually hers.

The woman in the ambulance is picking up the phone from the floor. She plugs it into a charger at their feet and waits a moment until the screen glows white. Then she swipes the lock screen while Taylor watches in a daze. "I see a contact for 'Dad' in your phone, sweetie. Hold on."

She doesn't hear what the woman is saying after that.

All she can hear is the bullhorn and the river of people streaming through the parking lot around them. She hears giggling. Gasps. A shriek. Someone crying. The unmistakable click of photos.

And screaming. Always screaming.

CHAPTER 51

Norah knows it's completely useless to continue clawing at the thin, impossibly strong ropes on Jamie's legs.

With the bloody nail still clenched between her fingers, she kneels on the ground between Jamie and the freckle-faced boy. She keeps her eyes fixed on the yellow rope, ignoring the red liquid that covers her hands and the floor.

She wants to run.

But she can't leave them.

Or him.

Behind her, she can hear the steady, low drone of his radio. It's still humming, just audible beneath the sound of Norah's own labored breathing as she digs at the knots in vain.

She nudges her shoulder upward to wipe at the sweat dripping down the side of her face. Then she turns again, to glance at the green square still blinking a few yards away.

The green square hasn't moved.

Somewhere beyond the maze, she can just hear the tinny bark of a bullhorn.

They're coming. Really coming.

She says it out loud to make it real, to make up for the fact that she hasn't managed to set any of the others free yet. "Help will be here any second," she whispers. Then repeats it louder. "They'll be here any second.

They don't have to be quiet anymore.

Soon, there are voices. The dim strobe of flashlights appears and grows brighter. The wail of a siren gets louder, and Norah hears tires skidding on dirt and gravel.

She feels the bubble of hysterical relief rise to the top of her throat as she runs a hand along Jamie's damp, matted hair, straining her eyes in the dark to see Aaron, who is lying a few feet away in the darkness.

Help is finally here—to take them away. To take *him* away.

Norah squints as the beams of light coming from outside the mill grow brighter, suddenly flooding the room in a blaze of light and noise. She hears footsteps as the lights circle chaotically before coming to rest on the boys, then Jamie, and then Norah herself.

Norah braces as some of the flashlight beams continue to trail along the floor, finding Maren and Ben.

Her hands clench as the flashlights trail over the red sawdust near the wall. She wills herself not to look away when the man's body appears.

There's no question it had to be done. But that doesn't change the fact that Norah was the one who did it. Or the fact that she wanted to do it.

One EMT helps Norah to her feet as two other EMTs kneel beside Jamie and the boys with a flurry of repetitive snips and murmured reassurances. Finally, Jamie's hands and then the boys' raw hands and ankles fall limp and bloody into the sawdust.

The first EMT is saying something, asking Norah questions. But Norah is still watching the flashlight beams that have come to rest in the bloody pool of sawdust, just shy of the gaping black doorway.

The softly burbling, green-lit radio is still clipped to the man's torn jacket, awash in dark blood.

Beneath the jacket, there is blood. So much blood.

But nothing else.

Norah blinks at the green-lit radio screen, feeling the floor tilt beneath her feet.

Have they already taken him away?

Even as the question materializes, she scans the dark room wildly, knowing that the answer is no. Bile rises in her throat as the relief recedes. She hears someone shout that they've found blood in the maze outside.

An officer wearing a black jacket appears through the shifting crush of shadows and flashlight beams. He crouches beside Jamie as an EMT attempts to peel away the tape that's wrapped around her mouth and head, asking a steady stream of questions before she can even speak.

Jamie whimpers when the EMT barks out a reprimand at the officer, and he reluctantly stands. "Jesus Christ," he mutters, glancing back at the dark doorway where more beams of light crisscross through the darkness beyond the mill.

The officer turns toward Norah, the contours of his face harsh in the dim beams of the flashlights' crossfire. She watches in a haze as he gestures toward the far side of the mill, where the bloody jacket and radio lay inanimate in the sawdust, a dark island in a pool of blood. "I know you all have been through hell, but we need to get started as quickly as possible if we're going to find him. Can you tell me what happened here?"

But even as Norah feels herself nod mutely, she knows she can't.

CHAPTER 52

December 15th

The cemetery in Rupert is small enough that Taylor can see Maren's grave from the frozen, nearly empty parking lot.

Jamie doesn't want to come here yet, despite her counselor's gentle, persistent encouragement. Taylor understands. Sometimes she doesn't actually get out of the car. But she can't stay away. If the Thicket were still open, she'd probably go back there too. Like Norah.

The idea of Maren's body lying tucked into the earth here makes her feel like she might pass out. But it's still something.

Ben was buried in Idaho Falls, an hour and a half away. Taylor didn't go to the funeral, and she hasn't visited his grave. Her name and face were plastered across SocialBuzz and the news in the weeks after it happened. Who knew what his parents might think of her. Or about Maren, whose photo is the focal point of every article. There is a photo making the rounds where Maren's face is hidden by the bloody sawdust, her legs splayed in opposite directions behind her, and the ribs of her corset still glowing faintly in the dark of the shack.

Taylor turns off the car engine and wraps her coat tight against the wind that whips her braid painfully into her neck as she steps out of the car. The flowers she's brought will be dead within a couple of hours.

When she reaches the modest, rounded headstone just beyond the flimsy gate, she stops. Dusted with a scuff of snow but still unfrozen is a handful of pale yellow daffodils.

Taylor glances around the empty cemetery warily, wondering who else was here to see Maren. Her eyes land on a gravestone two rows back, the mound of earth still not level with the ground.

Brandon Lewis. 2005-2019.

The same yellow flowers sit huddled beneath the headstone.

Through blurry eyes, Taylor trudges back to her car, her grief pinwheeling between confusion and gratitude. Then she sees the car door, twenty yards away, open a crack.

The girl's thick brown hair floats upward, framing her face in a dark halo as she attempts a smile before her expression crumples.

Taylor hesitates, then hurries the short distance to Norah's beat-up Buick and opens the passenger-side door.

Norah doesn't say anything. Or ask how she's doing.

Instead, she lets the tears flow down her cheeks without apologizing while they both look out over the scrubby cemetery, breathing in the lingering smell of daffodils.

CHAPTER 53

He clicks *refresh.*

He waits thirty seconds, then clicks again.

Two hundred and ten dollars. Twenty-two bids. Three days left.

Original production, 2018, the listing reads. *Exact model used in Thicket killings.*

There are twelve more listings just like it on eBay. He clicks to zoom and enlarges the image until the mask's black eyeholes fill the screen in front of him.

Unconsciously, he touches the dense web of stippled, still-ropy scars running in raised red crisscrosses across his neck, all the way up to his ears and down his sternum.

Despite his thick coat, she'd chipped his collarbone in several places. He can feel the sharp divots when he presses down on the wrecked skin covering his sternum.

Even though she was one strike away from hitting an artery, the memory brings with it a curious mix of exhilaration and loss.

He'd never been bathed in his own blood before.

A baptism, he thinks.

Or an atonement. For misjudging how the scales had tipped.

They have his DNA now. He knows that much. There was enough blood at the scene that some people speculate—even without a body for evidence—that he must be dead.

He feels confident he came close.

He felt it in the way his head spun as he crept through the sawdust in the dark along the wall, quietly extricating himself from the jacket—and the radio. He slipped out the door the girl had left open behind her as she ran.

He remembers the floating feeling and the way his breath came in gasps as he staggered through the outer maze. The numbness in his fingers spread to his arms then down his legs as his heart fought to keep his vital organs alive. As he crawled along the dark brush fringing the grassy lot, the red and blue lights from the emergency vehicles flashed in his peripheral vision, mingling with the dots floating in front of his eyes.

There was, of course, no hospital visit. He stitched the deepest lacerations himself then packed his wounds in gauze and compression bandages, knowing the rest would heal with enough time and a little luck.

His neighbor, the old woman next door, had brought him soup every other day for three weeks until the swelling went down and the lacerations scarred over. Each time, she clucked at his carelessness in biking without a helmet that dark October night. She insisted that she would bring her daughter by when he was healed up, so they could meet.

Each time the knock at the door came, he wondered if he would open it to find someone in uniform standing on his porch.

But it was always Janet. And with each passing day, each passing week, he feels more sure that he won't.

Caroline Tolley of Channel Two kept him company while he healed. The news coverage of the second "rash of murders" had been even better than the first. There was endless speculation and endless stories. There had even been an *Investigation Discovery* reenactment.

He refreshes the eBay listing again.

Still two hundred and ten.

He frowns, then opens a new tab. Craigslist: Gigs.

He's been cooped up inside his apartment for four weeks now.

Outside the window, in the entryway to the apartment complex, he can see that management has already strung a pathetic-looking straggle of multicolored Christmas lights.

He quickly scans the Craigslist listings, looking for signs that a job will be under-the-table pay.

After opening two promising leads in a new browser, he allows himself the indulgence of typing "The Thicket" into his browser.

He won't go back. He knows that.

Not there, anyway.

He feels a pang of impatience as the memories make his scars pulse hot.

Then he opens another anonymous browser and types "best haunted houses" into the search bar.

63,700,000 results.

It's too late this year.

But next year, they'll open again.

A NOTE FROM THE AUTHOR

If you enjoyed this book, a positive review would mean the world to me. Like other small-press authors, I rely heavily on word-of-mouth recommendations to reach new readers.

I can promise you that I read every single review. Because each one is a new window into this story. And because if you loved this book, *you're* the one I wrote it for—which is why I'm placing this note *before* the acknowledgments.

ACKNOWLEDGMENTS

A heartfelt thank-you to Jeanne Allen of Copyrank Composition for the many brainstorming sessions and the invaluable editing expertise.

Another big thank-you to Karen and Georgia of the *My Favorite Murder* podcast. Every episode feels like a "Take back the night" rally as you call out the creeps and guide the focus back to the survivors and victims who deserve a voice. SSDGM to all my murderinos.

And thank you to Nate, for being my first advance-reader, my home, and my best friend.

ABOUT THE AUTHOR

Noelle's two great passions are murder and horses (separately, never together).

Noelle is a boy-mom to Luke and Max, and a cat-mom to Michelle. When she's willing to wear pants (which is less often than she aspires to wear them), she can be found in mom jeans. Her husband Nate is the best person she knows.

Made in the USA
Las Vegas, NV
13 January 2022

41273581R10171